Night on the Invisible Sun

By Alec Bryan

Published by Aqueous Books, Watchtower
P.O. Box 12784
Pensacola, FL 32591

www.aqueousbooks.com

Published in the United States of America

ISBN: 978-0-9826734-2-3

First edition, Aqueous Books printing November 2010
Watchtower imprint
Chapters One through Three first appeared online serially in the literary journal
Prick of the Spindle.

Cover art and design, book layout: Cynthia Reeser

Acknowledgement: Excerpt from "CCLXXXVII. Ode on Intimations of
Immortality from Recollections of Early Childhood" by William
Wordsworth in the chapter "When Stars Die"

Aqueous Books

For Ron Deeter, a Doctor of Literature

Life is a pure flame, and we live by an invisible sun within us.
—*Sir Thomas Browne*

The exceeding brightness of this early sun
Makes me conceive how dark I have become.
—*Wallace Stevens*

TABLE OF CONTENTS

Tugs and Pulls of the Modern World

THE creature awoke. The shadowy remnants of the late afternoon's nightmare still formed a faint and incomprehensible outline in its mind. It tried to focus on the skeleton, but lost even the slightest trace of what was once there. Crouched in its enveloped darkness, shaky, wondering what this recurring dream might mean, the creature began by recollecting, in order, the things it knew with certainty: It knew, for sure, it was still alone, it was still trapped, and night was fast descending, and, in twilight's utter and solemn emptiness, and, in its nocturnal silence, it knew a strange voice penetrated the cocoon's outer wall and fell upon its prickly ears.

"Is anyone in there," asked the voice.

The small creature responded as resoundingly as something trapped can, and as loudly as a thing dares when it is not sure the voice—especially after its recurrent daymare—constitutes a reality beyond the constructs of its own inventive thinking. "Yes, I am in here," its echo reverberated throughout the cocoon.

The voice continued. "I have walked the forest many days this summer, and I noticed early on this cocoon, fully built, yet nothing has ever emerged. Why have you stayed locked in for such a long time, little creature?"

With its feeble comprehension, the creature was not able to alert the man that being in a cocoon is somewhat like being in a coma: One does not realize how long one has been comatose until summoned, and then the passage of time is only recognizable through exterior indicators. The creature replied with candor, "I apologize, but I do not have the power to break the casing I have constructed."

The man laughed heartily. "As a traveler, I have encountered many predicaments like yours before, little creature. Let me guess…you developed your wings, and in so doing have grown too big for your cocoon? It would be ideal if your strength had developed commensurate with your wings; then, you could burst through the covering's thin walls."

The creature replied, "If I had just a little room in which to move, with the slightest momentum I could force myself through this barrier, but it appears my rapid growth has hindered my escape. Is there anything I can do to get out? If you could condescend to help, I would be forever in your debt."

The little creature's honest and humble reply appealed to the man's altruistic nature. He knew precisely how to help the trapped creature escape its cocoon, but his method was neither painless nor conventional—as an escape rarely is. He explained that its release would come at a great and inevitably painful cost. But the creature was unable to think about or measure costs, and, desiring the simple liberties allotted unto others, told the man it did not worry about the price of freedom.

"Okay," said the man. "It's dark now. I will be back in the morning. Think about what I have told you, and if you still wish for your freedom when you wake, then I will help you achieve it. Until tomorrow, my trapped little creature."

With that, the man walked off through the forest, but, before leaving, turned once to mark the place where the cocoon hung, even though he had passed it numerous times, then went on his way. The creature pressed its ear to the cocoon and strained to hear each step of the old man's retreating feet, until even the sound of his quiet footfall was finally inaudible.

Aside from a random cricket's chirping, the creature was left once again to the utter solitude of night. But the dark did nothing to impede the creature from feeling excitement and anxiety over what had just happened; in fact, the night had the opposite effect. As it pondered its pending freedom, the creature could not help but think that its abode had never felt so alone and so dark, and, yet, at that very moment, the shroud of darkness never felt so much like a warm blanket. The creature experienced the same reluctance as a bird when it leaves the warmth and security of incubation for the ferocity of a cold birth. In life, only the moribund, roused and yet frightened by the clarion call from the unknown, could comprehend such peaceful and all-encompassing warmth and security of the already-known—for birth is the cousin to death.

II

The next morning the man was true to his word, his arrival coordinated with the earliest light bursting through the rheumy walls of the creature's cocoon.

"Good morning, little creature," said the man. "How did you sleep?" The creature admitted it slept heavily but soundly until morning, when it started to wonder whether the man would reappear.

"Ah, a natural reaction, little creature. When we think we are to pass on to something new, anxiety and doubt are the first uninvited guests knocking upon the confines of our frenzied mind's door. Luckily, anticipation resides deep within us and is a vigilant guardian of that door. It will not let transients stay long before it scurries them on their way. And, did you, little one, think about the proposition set before you?"

The creature replied with exuberance, "I have, and I have decided that a little pain presently caused is worth the end result of freedom."

"Ah, yes, present pain, but you misunderstood me, little one. Proximate pain oftentimes leads to a future fraught with constant suffering; it is the augmenting, not the assuaging thereof. Are you sure, and I mean absolutely positive, you want to be freed?"

The creature thought about its current situation and the lack of space for movement, the darkness and the silence, and decided that freedom at any cost would be better than living as it was. "I want to be freed, good sir, and I would be forever grateful if you could accommodate my request."

With shrugged shoulders and a slight gasp of air, the old man responded to the little creature's importuning through a somber yet somehow optimistic, "So be it. Let us begin."

Having the little creature retreat to the farthest corner (albeit not a great distance, due to the creature's size) of the cocoon, and with the precision of a surgeon operating on his miniature child, the old man pulled slowly on the single, loose-silk fiber pinched between his fingernails. As the fiber unwound about a foot or two, the man placed it in the center of a thick book and closed it, trapping the string-like fibril along the inner spine. The man then had the creature withdraw as far as possible within the cocoon, and he repeated the process as gingerly as possible—this time trapping the silk string along the spine of a slimmer book. Once accomplished, the man sat near the cocoon so his head was positioned right below the swaying branch. "Now, little creature, I want to read you a short passage from each of the two books; as I have employed their integral service in this process, I find it only fair to speak something of what lies within." Turning pages of the first book, the old man began telling his odd discourse *in medias res*:

"And not only so, but we glory in tribulations also: Knowing that tribulation worketh patience; and patience, experience, and experience, hope: And hope maketh not ashamed; because the love of God is shed abroad in our hearts."

Peculiar and foreign as the words were, they appealed to an innate part of the creature that had lain latent for so long that, as it acted up, it stung sharp as it burnt within. The man continued reading from what he called the "big book":

"Beloved, think it not strange concerning the fiery trial which is to try you, as though some strange thing happened unto you: But rejoice, inasmuch as ye are partakers…"

And on and on he continued. But the creature did not consciously comprehend anything else, for the part it remembered was sufficient to make its mind reel to and fro and unravel, creating a dreamlike state of consciousness. The words were too much for the little creature to take in one sitting. It was full and baffled by both the logic and illogic of the statements, and wondered what such things might signify.

The man suddenly stopped reading, then, after a pause, addressed the creature. "Well, little creature, what do you think of such a discourse?" Another pause, and lingering silence. "Do not answer, little one. I know. I know. Such things take time to develop into concrete thought. Ideas are born in liquid. Now, while you sit thinking, let me read to you from the slimmer book."

He grabbed the second book, and the fibrous silk wedge caught within it caused the branch to sway for a few moments. Opening the book, the man began with another strange, poignant address. The creature did not remember all the man read, but certain passages caused the same, singular burning sensation within its abdomen, only more visceral and accompanied by a caustic tinge. The lines unfurled thus:

"I know it; why not try this diversion? Ask every passenger on this ship to tell you his story, and if you find a single one who has not often cursed the day of his birth, who has not often told himself that he is the most miserable of men, then you may throw me overboard headfirst."

The rhetoric gathered impetus, and, around, it seemed to spin in the opposite direction of the man's first readings, all the while weaving, in vicious counterrevolutions, with each word, what the other book had unwoven.

"When his highness sends a ship to a foreign land, does he worry whether the mice on board are comfortable or not?"

And the strange address continued, but, like before, the creature's capacity to comprehend had already been reached, and its mind was wandering down distant labyrinthine paths and running into constricting walls.

And when the man stopped reading and the creature heard nothing but his rhythmic breathing, the creature felt a weight it never had before, and it began to question whether it had made a mistake in employing the man's services, for the woe of being was so attenuated by the discoursing, the creature considered freedom altogether a mistake. Perhaps a life of lethargy had its advantages. The creature's eyes clenched tight; a spectral silence enclosed its face. It must have sat this way for a long moment of time.

When finally the creature opened its eyes, expecting to see the same silky and soft envelope, it was shocked to discover that its chrysalis had completely unraveled and lay upon the branch, drooping hopelessly toward the forest floor. The creature was afraid, its natural reaction a shudder that ran from the tip of its ciliate antennae down through the base of its abdomen. It did not know what to do. Through dilated eyes it saw the forest to each side, the sky above, and, below, it recognized the ashen gray hair of the man who had set it free. It closed its eyes again. The reality of the extrinsic scene compared with the imagined outer world it had envisioned caused such a dichotomy that everything the creature now viewed possessed a vague sense of unreality. With a specific sense of fear creeping into its abdomen, a sinister concern arose, causing the creature to wonder if what it had just agreed to would cause a pain much more distinct and sharp than the joy of the freedom now allotted unto it.

At this moment, and discerning the creature's predicament, the man spoke. "Oh, no, little one, closing your eyes won't help. You cannot go back into the dark lair you once inhabited. It is gone forever. Shudder if you must, but this is life in its awful and irreversible splendor."

The man's words, harsh as they were, quelled the anxiety the creature was then feeling, and, sensing the adroitness in all the man had said and done thus far, the creature thought it prudent to ask him what it should do now that he had afforded it freedom. But without allowing the man time to respond, the creature was curious to see the books that were used as instruments in unraveling the small cocoon's silk casing, and asked where they were.

The man explained the process had taken longer than the creature may have surmised, and as he had thrown each book in an opposite direction with the stringy silk embedded deep in its spine, the cocoon unwound itself and parted on either side of the creature, leaving it precariously alone on the branch, much the way a sleeping fish would look upon waking if it were to find the lake it roved and prowled had dried up overnight.

"I will gather my books, now—they are not too far from here—and then I will be on my way. It is almost the season for me to begin my work again. I will not be able to return to the forest; therefore, I wish you luck, creature, in your endeavors."

The man, using the tree as a brace, struggled to his legs and peered at the creature askance with imploring eyes that spoke of a sadness the creature could not yet comprehend. The man wished the creature well one last time. In the throes of anxiety and fear, the creature tried to stall the man, afraid to see him leave, for the indecision as what to do next remained vexing. How was it to act?

"But wait, kind sir. Do not leave me, yet. I do not know what to do, where to go, or, for that matter, if I am even able to move!"

The old man paused, and whispered to the creature: "There is but one thing for you to do, little one—you attempt to fly."

The creature looked perplexed, as the man shuffled off a few feet and then turned once more and in an exhortatory tone offered his final advice of the day, "Before you go on any predisposed flight of fancy when you fly, for fly you will, be sure to fly straight up, not teeter-tottering to the left or the right, not vacillating forward or backward, but straight up until you have a wonderful view of all that surrounds you, and, as you hover, fluttering high above us down here, take in the immaculate sprawl of life, see what it is that lies around you, contemplate where you would like to go, and then begin your trek into whichever foreign region it is you wish to venture."

The man looked one more time at the creature and then ambled out of the forest. Meanwhile, the creature hollered a parting thanks to the man's back and then sat dejectedly upon its branch. The old man vanished through the stifling wall of black trees surrounding the creature, and, as he did, the poor creature thought to itself, *What will I do now*, and realized it had not even asked the man what kind of creature it was, nor had the man gathered his books before he hobbled off.

After composing itself for a period of time, and allowing its eyes to adjust to the unfiltered light, the creature flickered and fluttered its brittle wings to ensure they would move, and, in so doing, scuttled forward on the branch—its wings worked. The flapping motion was as natural as breathing; it was the physical exertion the creature was unaccustomed to. Resting for a moment, it decided it was ready to attempt flight. Flapping its wings in furious beats and letting go of the branch, it began its ascent. Ignorant of such levity, and with slightly atrophic strokes, the creature veered right and left, then forward and backward, as it climbed skyward.

Barring such accidental movements from the path on which the man had set the creature, it continued to climb higher, rising with each rhythmic beat, slowly gaining the cadence of flight as it passed the canopy of black trees. The creature noticed the lightness of the air, and with such attention came an easier ascent. Rapturously, the creature continued its climb as the fibrillations of its heart pounded unceasing. Nearing the giant cumulus mediocris clouds, the creature decided it had achieved the heights required to view its surroundings; any farther up and the clouds would obscure its view altogether. It looked down upon the terrestrial land. Much to its dismay, the anticipation of reaching such atmospheric heights had prepared it for a view congruent with the ecstasy of the climb and the proud quivering through its entire abdomen.

What it saw instead was how small, distant, and foreign the land appeared. The height distorted everything. The forest ran for miles, but it was just that—a simple forest. Typical cottages were scattered throughout, but there was nothing unique about them. Off in the distance a jagged but common mountain range rose, and in the other direction a large river meandered through a valley, but the creature saw nothing out of the ordinary, and nothing resembling life. From such heights, the entire scene resembled a cheap, one-dimensional image painted by an artist who could not fathom the disparate depths of the incongruous peaks and valleys and crags and crevices any more than a stick-figure drawing of a family could capture the intricacies taking place within each member's mind, or the delicate and subtle nuances that made the family unique.

The creature had expected something more from such soaring heights, yet all it had found was a groping kind of solitude and a fractured view of flight, and an indomitable longing to be back amid the multi-dimensional world about which it knew so little. It suddenly grew sick of the elevation it had reached; the space in its breast, once filled with rapture toward the climb, first turned hollow, and then quickly began again to fill. Only, this time, it inflated with what felt like leaden weights, accompanied by a heavy nausea.

The enervated creature decided it had seen enough. It immediately began its descent, and, much like the climb, aimed straight down, veering very little to the left or right or backward or forward. It quickly fell toward the canopy of trees and then maneuvered its way through the branches and leaves protruding outward in an intricate web of green and brown limbs. In the denser air, the creature glided effortlessly, alighting on the same branch it had earlier left. The creature perched upon the branch and waited for the nauseating effects of its flight to depart, sitting for hours with its head pounding and its heart filled with a new pang similar to the one felt earlier in the day, only throbbing louder. The pang did not seem to stop in the center of its abdomen, but ventured its way into every extremity, including its head and antennae.

As the creature sat, it felt the cold, depressing wind against its back, and, for the first time, remembered the warmth of its cocoon and the melodious sound the wind had made as it beat upon its once-immutable shell. While it pondered such things, the creature felt a loneliness it had never experienced; so real and so powerful was this new melancholy that in its stupefied state the creature tried to reconstruct its cocoon with the remains of the strung-out silk still clinging to the branch. But its efforts were futile, for the string was unraveled, and, try as the creature might, it could not cover its flanks in the incessant wind. Throughout the day, paralyzed and quasi-catatonic, the creature sat upon the branch. It remained cold and disheartened as darkness descended. With the advent of night, each new gust of haunting wind sounded like the howl of some nefarious demon come to wreak havoc upon the exposed and vulnerable creature. What had its freedom sprung upon it?

The creature did not sleep.

III

As the nascent sun began to extend its breath of vitality through the wall of trees, the forest yawned to life; simultaneously, the wind and the strange noises from the night before began their recession, and, for all the force the dominion of dark carried with it during the night, its morning retreat marked a hushed and acquiescent farewell. When a child closes his eyes to receive the poke of the needle, the child keeps his eyelids clamped and muscles tensed in expectation that the needle's retraction will prove just as sharp and painful as its entry, and only upon opening his eyes does the child realize the needle has already been withdrawn. This painless retraction from his flesh emboldens the child to express, "It was not that bad." Day arrives in similar fashion, and with similar results. In hindsight, it would be ridiculous for the child to call the needle evil just because it inflicted a temporary pain; so, too, the night deserved no derision from the creature.

Ecstatic it had made it through the frightful night still clinging to life, the creature arrived at the conclusion that perhaps its freedom might prove worthwhile. Nevertheless, it did not wish to suffer through another night. It decided on a rapid course of action—to find the man who had set it free. What it would do once it found the man never crossed its callow mind. And, so, judging by the direction in which the man had hobbled off, the creature took to the sky for a second time and headed east.

After a week of fruitless searching, sleeping on windowsills—the light and afterglow of warmth escaping the homes pleasant in contrast to the bleak darkness the forest had presented that first night—the creature began to think its journey hopeless. In its fits of despair, however, near the outskirts of town, it espied a man carrying a shovel caked with dirt. Even from a distance, the creature recognized the slight, doddering steps. The creature immediately fluttered in the old man's direction, and, upon closer inspection, realized it had indeed found the man for whom it had been searching. Not knowing how to broach a conversation and feeling awkward in its hovering silence, the creature asked the first question that entered its head, "Where are you going?"

"From where I came, eventually," replied the perambulating old man.

The creature thought about the man's response, and, after a pause of consternation, caught up to him and asked if it could come along. The man suffered the creature to tag along, and, so, not knowing where it would be taken and exhausted from flight, the creature settled on the man's dirty shoulder.

"So, this is what you have decided to do with your freedom, eh? Accompany a decrepit old man."

The creature did not know how to respond. For the time being, it let silence prevail. The old man ambled through the town, giving nods of affirmation to passersby, but receiving little or no response in return. Once the old man left the town's bustle behind, the creature asked what he planned to do with the shovel. The old man did not respond, but rather continued to walk on in silence. The creature mistook the old man's non-responsiveness as evidence he had not heard the question. "What will you do with the shovel you carry?" it repeated.

The old man's aberrant response stunned the creature. "I will do with the shovel what the shovel was made to do. I will dig. I will dig a hole—a hole so deep I will either come out on the other side, creating a tunnel of light through the hollow earth, or I will strike fire at the center, and, thus, travel no farther."

The creature laughed a little at the man's odd response until the old man's discerning eyes rested their penetrating gaze upon it, and only then did the creature cease its chortling and realize with reproach the man had heard it. It is a strange embarrassment evoked when a topic of extreme seriousness is mistaken for a subject of naught. The awkwardness is not felt because of an oversight on the perpetrator's part, but rather for the complacency with which the offended views the topic in question. How could the old man not know such a response was preposterous?

"Why?" asked the perplexed creature. "Why a hole?"

"I see I must explain everything to you. Very well, then."

The man explained that when he was a young boy, he used to help his father dig holes. But the holes were only six-feet deep and once the old man (then a young boy) reached the six feet, he always experienced an unsatisfied, itching feeling that perhaps he should go deeper. Six feet was where the dead lay. He wanted to go beneath the shallow surface and to the bottom of it all.

"You see, little creature, when I was young, I did not know what compelled such strange desires. Now, I know. And what was then taken for a child's whim has become the driving force of my old age."

"What have you discovered with age that has changed your perspective on digging holes?" asked the creature.

"It is not easy to explain to you, little one, but I will try."

With his humble introduction, the old man began his first attempt of many to recapitulate the past and capture, with veracity, the essence, all the while failing to avoid the temptation of extracting didacticism.

IV

"My father was a gravedigger. Once I was old enough to wield a shovel, I began working alongside him. After digging holes for a year or so, I asked him why he had become a gravedigger. My father replied he did not choose such a morose profession, but stumbled upon it when my mother became pregnant and he was unemployed. 'Simply to make ends meet,' he said. 'We were in a bind, and I needed to make sure your mother was provided for. 'But,' he continued, 'I have since learned a valuable lesson from this job. I have learned that to have a finger on the pulse of humanity, you must also have one foot in the grave, Son.'

He went back to work and did not speak another word to me that afternoon. At the time, I did not put much stock in his saying. I suppose it just sort of slipped into my unconscious and lingered.

Anyway, my father and I used to come home from a hard day's work, and my father would not say much, but my mother knew the routine: Someone had died, and needed to be buried. Such was the nature of our job. As it was my father and I who would do the digging for the town, we would stand at a distance as the procession made its way to the hole, and we could not help but overhear someone say nice things about the deceased. It didn't matter if the person deserved such praise while living; he got it when he was dead. Then, the person doing the eulogizing would move to the family's regrets due to a lack of time spent with the now-deceased. A son would say there was no time to throw a ball with his father. A daughter would lament the lack of time he had to take her to the fair or help her with her schoolwork. A wife would sob over all those promised trips, all those sights they had wanted to see together, if she could just hold off a few more years until he retired. But now he was eternally retired, and the gulf between the living and the dead is impassable. My father would stand and listen, and he could not help but think of the finality of death, like a cut cord never to be strung back together, because once severed, the lost tension in the cords caused them to fly in separate directions. My father and I would wait for the family to leave, and then we would bury the deceased, covering him forever with a smattering of dirt, allowing the man to decompose in peace.

My father and I would not wash when we got home. He used to say to me, 'You leave the dirt on those hands. It is time to eat.' He would sit at the table and eat like he had never eaten before. He would scarf down his food with as much refinement as a pack of wolves devouring a dead animal. He would breathe loudly, and food would spill from the sides of his mouth, and he would grab his water and gulp it down and let it run over his chin. Then, he would set the cup down and wipe his face with his dirty hands. The family would watch his communion in profound silence. Hardly a word was spoken.

After the ritual, he would take a bucket of water and the lye soap, and he would clean off the dirt and grime that had worked its way underneath his fingernails, behind his ears, into his hair, and any other place dirt manages to hide. After washing, he would come back downstairs, cleansed, like a new man, and would play with the younger kids, and he had this look in his eye like it was the first time he had ever played with them, as if they had just been removed from the womb and handed over by a midwife, and he was so happy to see they were alive and breathing. The wonderment in his eyes, creature; you should have seen it. It was as if every day he watched the procession of death it resurrected him, and this resurrection was his life—he didn't want to wait for the next. He feared the irrevocability of death he saw in the drawn-out faces, in the eyes of the living, at those funerals."

The now-old man looked at the creature and said, "That statement of my father's, about one foot in the grave helping him keep a finger on the pulse of humanity, has not left me. It has grown in relevance over the years. In fact, it made me realize that I, too, love to dig. What my father chose as a profession because of my birth I have willfully inherited as his son."

The man abruptly stopped walking, swung the head of his shovel around, and began to dig.

Although the creature enjoyed hearing the old man reminisce, it remained aggravated. The man had not really answered its question. It was about to ask him more on the relevancy of digging holes, but perplexed as to why the man chose such a location, asked him, instead, "Why have you chosen this spot?"

"Because, my prying little one, as the world is round, it does not matter where one starts to dig a hole. The digger is the axis, is the auger, and, as long as the digger keeps at it, he will either reach the fiery center that lights the earth and grants it life, or he will tunnel through the center and break through to light on the other side."

The creature sat on the man's shoulder and stewed over his strange course of action. It was perplexed. It wondered just how stable the old man was, and it wondered whether it was safe to stay at his side. But, it could not abandon him. The man had been its source of freedom, and the creature felt a kindredness reverberating far beyond the boundaries of its comprehension.

The man, taking a brief respite from his digging, leaned against his shovel, and, once again with his intuitive nature, ascertained what the creature was thinking. "You question the validity of such a quest, do you? Well, let me tell you another story of my youth."

And, in an attempt to further recapitulate the past, the man delved into another anecdote, while the creature sat in silence.

V

"When I was a boy, I had a bird. The bird loved to sing. Our house resounded with its immaculate chirps and warbles each morning and on through the day. I listened for hours in my room as I read or studied. Its chirping was, to me, the most sonorous, comforting, and joyful of sounds. One day, however, the bird stopped. This befuddled me. I knew its silence was not because it had grown old, for, purchased when a fledgling, the bird still had five or six years to live. I thought its silence might be due to failing health, but then decided, 'No, it's not its health, because the bird still eats.' I knew it was not the wings, because they never were clipped. I then realized it must be the blasted cage; the cage was stifling the bird's spirit. I rationalized that if I were locked in a cage and able to behold, nay, grasp, through the bars that kept me shut in, the very freedom denied me, my spirits would be quashed as well.

The next day, the bird again refused to sing. Much to my chagrin, I decided to let it go free. So, with bitter resentment, I opened the cage. The bird stood statuesque on its little perch and refused to fly away. I tried coaxing it, letting it know it was free, saying the things a kid would: 'Come on, little birdie, you are free, now.' The bird would not go. Finally, I tried *shooing* it to freedom by putting my hand into its cage and forcing it toward the open door, to which the bird committed its only act of aggression—it bit me. It reached down with its tiny beak and pecked me hard enough to draw a small speck of blood where my skin meets my thumbnail. I felt the simultaneous emotions of shame and anger; I slammed the cage door shut and stormed from the room.

After bandaging my wound and allowing my anger to subside, I realized it was I who should be ashamed for having fallaciously surmised I could grant the bird its freedom by compulsory means. I rationalized that if my parents, through obligation, goaded me toward some objective, even if the objective resulted in an outcome I had hoped for, I would not be satisfied once it was obtained because my free will would have been manipulated in the process. The bird did not fly away because I was forcing it; if the bird wanted to leave, it would leave of its own volition and on its own terms. The bird would wait for the opportune time and then it would make its escape. So, I left the cage door open and stayed out of the room for a couple of hours, allowing the bird its opportunity to leave.

I returned later in the day and discovered the cage door shut, the bird still locked in. I figured a gust of wind must have slammed the cage door closed. I moved the cage away from the current of wind passing from window to window. This time, I tied the cage door open with a short piece of yarn and again left. I returned a few hours later only to find the door once again shut. The yarn lay on the ground, pecked to shreds. The bird sat upon its perch, staring at me. That was the last time I tried to open the cage. I never heard the bird sing again. Two weeks after these incidents, the bird died during the night. In the morning, I found it lying stiff in its own excrement at the bottom of its cage. We never knew for certain what caused its death.

Now, creature, I have thought long and hard about the bird's tragic demise, and, although as a boy I was enthralled by its singing, as an old man it is the bird's last days that fill me with wonder. I sit up late and marvel at what drove it to such madness; what possessed it to stay locked up, rather than enjoy its final fleeting hours; why it would silently suffer in its self-imposed cage and die."

The man paused, and, leaning on the shovel, seemed lost in reverie. The creature reflected as well. It still thought this man, the only man it had ever known intimately, was the strangest it would ever meet, but the question occupying the creature's anxious mind had nothing to do with the bird. Its preoccupation was simply remembering the hollowness of its cocoon, and wondering what the old man would do if the center of the earth was also hollow. The creature pictured the man breaking through the crust of the final, inner layer, and plummeting to his death. *The poor old man*, it thought. *What a meaningless journey if the center of the earth is hollow, or if it is so obdurate and compacted as he gets deeper that it renders his shovel useless.*

The man emerged from his stupor and looked at the creature sitting perfunctorily on his shoulder. "Give it time, creature. You will come not only to grasp my senseless journey, but you will come to wish you could do more to help. It is in your nature."

The creature did not respond. It wondered why it felt so drawn to a man destined to waste his life.

The man began digging again, making first a giant swath, methodically circling like a field sprinkler, then, with slow and calculated steps, maneuvered inward. Once he reached the center, he buried the shovel head into the earth at a steep gradient and formed a small hole, resembling the center mark of a protracted circle. Then, the man reversed the process of digging and worked toward the outer wall in expanding spirals.

While the man worked thus, the creature brooded. It was not satisfied with the old man's responses, and as it thought over what the man had said, it continued to harp on the man's ridiculous journey. "Why, again, are you digging a hole? Isn't there something else you could be doing?"

The man laughed as he piled shovelful after shovelful of excavated dirt outside the hole. He figured it was time to probe the depths of the poor creature's lack of understanding.

"Let me attempt to explain myself in an abstract way. Perhaps, creature, it is simply this: It is easy to understand life when it goes well. I have yet to hear a happy person complain of their happiness. True, they will complain of the transitory nature of happiness, but at the core of their lament is the wish for more elusive joy. However, when life goes sour—and it is a matter of when, not if—and when that sourness is needlessly brought about, it is more difficult to understand the irony of suffering. Now, I am still under the impression most suffering is needless. You will be hard-pressed to find a man who has survived the brutality of a war, the depravation of a prison cell, or the pangs of unrequited or adulterous love, and claims they are better for having gone through the furnace of such affliction. In each of these cases, an argument can be made that man is at the root of, the fundamental cause of, suffering's needlessness. I think it would be safe to say the causalities of most wars stem from the petty disagreement of men who spout off prideful denunciations of the diverging party's beliefs, or the irreconcilable differences between them, or the jockeying for geographical supremacy.

Oftentimes, war is nothing more than an extenuation of a neighborhood bully's lashing out just to prove he can. And the prisons of war are an extended function of the disagreement that caused the war. Now, these other prisons, the ones used to punish or *rehabilitate* the common criminal, are filled with men who are there because of their own vile actions. Love, as well, is a choice. True, you do not choose who you love—it seems to be biologically or geographically determined, and oftentimes goes against our rationale—but a lover does decide whether or not they will pursue that love and determines what the possible costs of that affection might be. If they did not, in advance, wager all the heartache and turmoil love would cost, it is safe to say it was an ill-advised future provision. Does everything I have said thus far ring true?"

"I suppose it is true," mumbled the creature, its misgivings locked within.

"Then, let us continue. Only, now, I must leave the subject's summer suppositions and venture into its wintry weather. I hope you have the capacity to follow.

There is another kind of suffering that is not brought on by man's relation to man, or his relation to nature, but rather is a self-imposed suffering caused by the irrationality of man's own mind. We produce this atypical type of suffering, and manipulate our lives to experience it at times—like the bird I had as a child. We say to ourselves, 'I suffer because I am good and will not give in.' Or, we say to ourselves, 'I suffer because I am not good enough and I deserve to suffer because I have chosen erroneously and must perform penance.' Why do we inflict pain upon ourselves? It is this type of unnecessary suffering that I believe we must come to understand, creature.

Life appears to be a balancing act between two opposing weights, and the final resting place of the voluntary carrier of the cross, or the one dragged down by the chains of hell, is down in the dirt; the only difference being in how one arrives at such a depth. And, if we view life in these terms, life, to a degree, becomes a quest of discerning which weight is dragging us down. Is it the chains of hell or the cross of burden that brings us here, or is each a sham? Either way, it is into the dirt that one must go to understand such things; one must dig. One must exhume the answers from the earth's very bowels. Perhaps, we discover that the truth of dirt weighs more than the truth of air? Is sorrow simply a taskmaster demanding more than frivolity? And since the obvious answer is *yes* in both cases, we must then ask, *why?*

It is easy, creature, to extract meaning from the lightness of love and happiness, but compressed underneath the rocks of oppression, depression, and lamentation, such meaning is hard to find; yet, these are the depths at which man works out his life. To fathom the reasons why sorrow exists and man pursues it—this, creature, is a worthy quest. To be able to pull a strand, exhume a grain of light or truth out of the pit of darkness—this, little one, is a quest worth losing one's life for. I now understand my father's saying, 'the story is in the soil.' All that has lived and died, and all that will yet live, is right here in the dirt. All that lives now and seeks to find meaning in life must dig past the brittle crust of suffering and arrive where the clay is always hard and speaks of the ironic nature of the true sufferer. Only then, in reverence, will life offer any of its mystery."

Once the man again rested his head on the shovel handle and the creature was sure he was finished with his story, the creature told the man he was crazy, that he had lost touch with reality, that the bird had something wrong with it, which was why it did not fly away. The creature shared in haste the things pressing upon its mind. But, once it unburdened itself, it realized it had not spoken with discretion and that the man was offended.

The man looked at the creature with disgust, and, with a slight inflection of vehemence, responded, "Did the bird have something wrong with it? Did it, really? Well, let me ask you something, creature," his tone now reaching a state of agitation: "During that first day of freedom, why did you try to go back to your cocoon?"

The creature was a little abashed by the man's query. It had not told him it returned to its cocoon.

"Why did you not openly embrace and relish your newfound freedom when it was granted to you?"

The man continued to lightly deride the poor creature, "Why have you not flown above the tree line since that first day? Did the lightness feel inhumane? Did the ease of your ascent make you sick; make you feel detached from life?"

31

The creature sat disconsolate. It did not know how to answer a man who had so easily discerned its actions. The man did not allow the creature much time to reply, but rather delved into another of his childhood stories. The creature was beginning to like the old man's stories less and less.

VI

"I had a neighbor I knew very well. We grew up together. We got into the same kind of trouble, laughed at the same kind of ribald joke, struggled through the same horrible lessons of arithmetic and grammar. Indeed, one could say we were quite similar. The boy was well-liked, good in sports, of a healthy disposition and a jovial spirit. These qualities endeared him to all who knew him. Well, one day our two families and some others from our small town went to the lakeshore to enjoy the blissful August sun. The boy decided he would go for a swim. Mind you, we weren't very old, maybe six or seven or at the most eight, and, therefore, his mother's maternal instinct was still on alert. The boy swam out past the usual marker, and instantly the mother, concerned, yelled, 'Son, son, don't you go out any farther, you hear me! You'll drown.'

The boy, treading water, head bobbing up and down, turned back to the shore, looked at us, then out toward the middle of the lake, looked back to us again, and yelled out, 'How do I know I will drown unless I keep going?' The other families, especially those with boys along the shore, lightly chuckled. The parents were glad their sons weren't as stubborn or brash as this child. The boy looked to the shore again, and then repeated his turn toward the middle of the lake, like the lake was luring him, as if some immense magnetic force lay at the center and his heart was a metal ball. He turned back around, and, with his head still bobbing slightly from the somber waves, yelled to the shore, 'I want to swim in deep waters, Mother.' He turned his head, and, with his back to us, facing the deeper waters he longed for, swam on, possessed with purpose.

Those on shore, especially his mother, began begging him to come back, but the boy would not heed such calls. He kept swimming as if it were his destiny to reach whatever lay in the lake's deep waters. The calls became more earnest, but to no avail. When they finally realized the boy would not consider their hollers, two older men, strong swimmers, plunged into the cool waters and swam after him. But there was no catching him. By the time they reached where he was when he yelled back to the shore, he had become a speck on the horizon. We spectators grew worried. We wondered why he would disobey his mother, why he would keep swimming when he knew the dangers such a far swim would entail.

As he proceeded farther out, our anxiety and worry increased. Finally, we lost sight of him altogether. He must have been dragged under the water's surface, must have felt the pull as he neared the center, and succumbed. We scoured and scoured the horizon, hoping to find any disruption along the plumb line, wishing any disturbance was him, but our hope was in vain. By the time three small rowboats were employed to aid the dismal search team, no hope lingered in our breasts that the boy would be found alive. And he wasn't. Weeks later, his bloated body was discovered floating face-down with the flotsam near the outlet of the lake. It was a tragic end to a tragic few weeks, and the weeks it took to find him didn't soften the blow for the family when they received the calamitous yet expected news. We could not share their grief. Our condolences seemed trite to them, and they did to us, too, but what can one do to assuage the bereavement of others when one does not suffer from the same hollow pang? Compassion does cause, to a degree, even the one who has not suffered to assume some of the pain for the family, but still an arbitrary gulf between the town's inhabitants, who still had their children, and the family, who had lost their only child, existed. The family moved away several months after, claiming the townspeople's faces served as a vigilant reminder of their loss.

Now, little creature, what possibly could have compelled the boy to abandon all rationale and plunge headlong into the depths of death itself? Why would he seek such a miserable lot? Was it miserable? And why is it that when people know they are going to die, they get such satisfaction from the simple rote of everyday living? Why don't they go somewhere, see the world, and fulfill last wishes before they die? Did the bird suffer more because it chose to stay, or did it serve as some innate stimuli, the workings of which lie within us and cause us, or the impetus carries us against common sense and the own goodness of our being, to seek out such experiences in our extremities? Was the bird living a life of deviation because it chose to face the awful reality one faces before death, or is everyone else living deflected, masked lives—lives that hide from pain, and pretend sorrow does not exist?"

The man faced the creature, and with a blank expression, repeated the question it had asked him so many times, "Why do I dig? Why do I dig? Why do I dig?"

He regained a semblance of composure, but continued unloading his tongue of the massive weight it had procured through so many years of solitude. "I ask you, creature, the same question in a different way: Why isn't more of the world digging? Why don't more people attempt to come to terms with the human experience? So many walk around as brain-dead zombies, mummified in visions of a false reality presented to them for their daily fix of vanity or any other of this century's anesthesia; each zombie willing to try anything to deaden the senses, and each as unwilling to dig up the dirt, to unbury the sorrow that, painful as it might be, alerts us that we are alive. Sure, creature, my life might be miserable, but at least at the bottom of my misery I am beginning to realize I am alive, and it is here, in the midst of my pit, that I find life most unadulterated and livable. And, no matter how painful knowledge of my predicament is, I would not trade it for the most luxurious anesthetic this world is capable of producing. No false ambrosia can erase the…"

The old man paused, mid-sentence. He looked again at the creature. A sense of empathy now revealed itself on the man's face. No longer haranguing the creature, and in an amicable tone, the man spoke with the calmness of a guru to a guileless disciple. "I suppose, creature, there are degrees of suffering, or different types of suffering, and some of these seem to serve a purpose. It appears suffering is the great teacher, and the lessons vary with the person. Suffering is the litmus test of mortality, and, when applied, some grow calloused, bitter, and angry at their lot in life; others grow humble, patient, and full of faith; yet others experience both poles, but walk their middle ground, neither hot nor cold—simply indifferent. I do not know exactly what this lesson or test is, and I do not claim to understand the purpose of suffering, so, I keep digging, looking for light on the other side of this darkness or hoping to strike it at the core, hoping beyond hope that a 'light might shine in darkness, and the darkness will comprehend it not'; praying with a heavy heart that I am not darkness, thinking lately I am both the darkness and the light."

The man's lecture was not over, but his energy had fizzled and he stopped speaking, even though the unsaid words lay heavy on his heart and mind. The creature was saddened by the man's melancholic demeanor and hoped to console him, but did not know what to say. With neither of them knowing how to comfort the other, the man again began digging, and the creature perched upon his shoulder to watch.

VII

After weeks of digging (much had been accomplished due to the porosity of the soil and the help of a wheelbarrow, which the man obtained the third day), the man, invigorated by his progress, deigned it necessary to impart his philosophy on how to dig a hole. He explained that the cardinal rule in hole-digging was to always leave a way out before you dig too deep.

"I learned a valuable and unforgettable lesson early in my career," the old man acknowledged. "Let me tell you one more story from my youth."

"Here we go, again," muttered the creature under its breath.

"In the vivacity of my youth, without forethought or method, overcome by my urge to dig, I began digging willy-nilly. I dug and dug with the voraciousness and single-mindedness only youth or the obsessed can employ. Before long, I realized I could only go so deep without running into problems. I heaved the shovelfuls up and out of the pit, but rapidly the distance became too great even for me, with my youthful virility, to muster, and eventually the dirt came crashing back upon my head. I had dug about twenty-feet deep before I realized my predicament. I had reached an impasse. I could dig no farther, and, as the light of day was fading, I began to fear I could not climb out of the pit. So, I ventured to scale the pit's walls, but the gradient was too steep and the edges were too far apart for me to shimmy my way up, and, when I tried, the dirt began to crumble under the weight of my hands and feet, causing me to slide back down.

After twenty minutes of my futile attempts to scale the pit walls, the waning light turned dimmer, and the darkness of the pit grew eerie. I began to fear the way little boys do—absolutely—and thought no perceivable light would reach me, and I would be forced to see out the night in utter darkness. Such desperate fear gripped me, and, instead of inciting a resourcefulness within, which would have allowed me to take my shovel and collapse one of the walls and pile up the caved-in dirt, the onslaught of darkness caused such anxiety that my mind ceased to function in a rational manner. The final light from the fading day dimmed and then went completely out, and on a starless night I thought how awful it was that I caused my own oblivion. I began to wail in anger at what a foolish boy I was, screaming, 'Why? Why did I do this?' I pictured myself, soul and all, disintegrating into the cloak of darkness surrounding me.

It was in this moment of excruciating anguish and despair that I thought I heard a voice. Two villagers, having worked later than expected in a nearby field, happened to be passing the hole, and must have heard my whimpers. Shining their light toward the pit's vicinity, the men saw the hole that had been dug and the pile of discarded dirt lying around it. They walked toward the pit, and, casting light over its lip, looked down. To me, light served as a sentinel, and the two villagers' outline could not have been more welcome had it been two messengers sent from the heavens. The men looked at each other askance, perhaps wondering if they had stumbled upon some modern biblical outcast thrown into the pit by jealous brothers, but there was no coat, and they knew by the pile of dirt and the shovel that the pit was probably of my own making.

Rather than asking what had happened, the older of the two men told me to wait as he ran to town to retrieve a ladder. I kindly thanked him, and, as he left, the other sat down, his feet and the lantern hanging over the pit's edge. The man asked what I was doing in a pit. I was ashamed of my stupidity, but so overcome by the reality I was safe that I grew bold and told the man about my urge to dig. You see, back then I did not know why I dug. I knew I had no answer that would satisfy the man's curiosity, so I told the truth. I told him I did not know why I was digging, other than I experienced the urge. No sooner had the words left my mouth than I realized how ridiculous I sounded. But the man did not admonish me; rather, he told me if I were to venture again to dig such a hole, to leave a way out.

The other man returned shortly thereafter and lowered the ladder to the bottom of the pit. I clung to each rung as I ascended; upon reaching the top of my pit, the younger man extended his arm. He then patted me on the back and commented how silly a boy I had been. I graciously thanked them, and, as the night was growing late, they told me I had better return to my family, who would be worried. The three of us parted company as abruptly as we had met.

And now, creature, that I am an old man, no longer shackled with the impulsiveness of youth, I have my wheelbarrow and I proceed to make a small spiral walkway along the outer edge of the hole. I always leave a way out. This, little one, is how a hole is properly dug." The creature laughed.

VIII

The man continued to dig, and, over time, the creature came to enjoy the process just as much as the old man. It enthralled the creature to watch the man, using the sharp point of his shovel, mark a line in the dirt wall where he would begin his day's digging. The creature would marvel, as during the day the line became higher and higher and the distance between it and the creature farther and farther. The man's pace was extraordinary, and as toilsome and tedious as the job might have been, his pace never seemed to lessen. That is not to say the digging did not exact a physical toll, for the man grew pale and his skin began to droop and sag; it had become emaciated, and no longer possessed the semi-tautness or elasticity even of middle age. His eyes still held their piercing capability, but so sunken and deeply withdrawn were those orbs, one would have had to look directly at them when the man was not moving to spot his pupils. And on top of all the physical reductions, the man's entire visage was besmeared with a film of dirt, lending him the appearance of a coal miner. He was physically hampered, yes, but mentally and spiritually the man stayed strong and maintained a steadfast pace that might have made the ancient rock roller himself jealous.

Then, the season began to change and the days waxed colder, and the light turned feeble and the man more somber. If a creature were capable of a look of disquietude, a furrowing of its brow a possibility, both would have served as proper indications for the feelings troubling the pitiable thing. The creature was concerned about the man's sudden slackening of pace. It wondered why he relented in his digging.

"It is nothing," the man retorted with an air of unease and doubt when asked. "It's just that I seem to get to this point and the work becomes painstakingly hard; I grow tired. This soil is not the light, silty loam we started with, creature; it is weighty, obdurate clay, compressed by the load of time and the pressure of earth. It is not easy to move."

The old man took a break and the creature, as had become customary, roosted upon his shoulder in an effort to buoy him. Also customary, the creature began asking the man too many questions. Only, on this day, the burden of being and the heft of his task pressed so heavily upon his shoulders and heart that the old man felt no need to shelter his irritability from the creature.

The callow creature asked the man for what seemed liked the tenth time of the day why he was convinced the creature would feel impelled to tell the world his story—as of late, this was a recurrent theme. The man was convinced the creature would leave him and venture out into the world. The creature would then counter that it would not leave his side, but would remain loyal to the end of the task.

However, on this day, it caught the man with his guard down; the man without malicious intent, but also lacking the forbearance that defined him, turned to the creature, and, reaching guttural tones of pity, said "You will leave me, and you will tell my story, because you do not know what else to do."

The man paused, as if seeking to regain composure, but, in reality, breathed in deeper to continue his frantic pace of unburdening. "It is your nature to live a life of quiet conflict against yourself. Born a caterpillar, you cling to the earth. The dirt is your abode, your protection; it is your mother. But then your transformation takes place and you climb into a tree, lock yourself up for a time, and emerge from your second birth displaying your new wings. The sky is your new home, and the light your newest longing, but it never can fully replace your wish to return to your first mother.

Many falsely believe this is why your kind attacks the light. You are angry at being ripped away from your first home, and, unable to return, you wage warfare against the source of all life. You miss your mother. You wish to return to her and tell her of your struggles. You hate your transformation. You curse life. Yes, this is what many believe: The scorned moth hates the light. I do not believe this," said the old man. "I believe the metamorphosed moth loves the light, but can never really embrace its new love the way it wishes, nor can the moth quite shed the habits of its first birth. Memory of its origins stay locked within."

Taking in another deep breath, the old man continued at a rabid pace: "I remember, growing up, how I used to enjoy seeing a moth enter a lamp-lit room on a summer's night and watch as it made love or waged war, however one chooses to view it, with the glowing light bulb; each pass would cast gigantic shadows upon the wall of the adumbrated moth. It was as if I were watching the extrinsic story of its life being told as the moth clung to the light, and, yet, if I turned to the wall, the inner struggle was projected as the penumbra writhed in spasmodic convulsions against the white.

It was as if the shadow was the old self caged within, still trying to write its story, almost like the moth heeded the light in an attempt to forever rid itself of its shadow by burning it, but I am unsure if this is what its action meant. And then the moth would either leave as abruptly as it entered and the walls would seem so stark, like blank pages of a story waiting to be written in comparison to how vibrant they were when the wings created shadows, or the moth would waste its ethereal life through its uncanny attraction to the light, burning its wings in its futile attempts at merging with the illumination, and, in silence, it would fall to the ground to flicker out its final moments in a spasm of twitches and turns. What a fate for a creature like you. The very thing you love and the very thing granting you life is also the source of your certain demise. There is an awful beauty in this death. No, creature. You will not stay down here much longer. You will venture into the light before it's too late."

The man was finished. He had shattered the remains of any cocoon-like stage for the moth, which found itself face-to-face with reality. And the creature, for its part, shouldered the load of what it had been told. At first, it refused to believe what the man had said, clinging to the belief that it was a butterfly and its adamant denial that it was a creature destined to die prematurely. Next, it experienced anger over the man's blunt and hurtful ravings. The dejected creature fluttered, and, finding no real corner in which to hide, landed near the edge farthest away from the man, hiding its sullen face behind its wings and tenebrously wailing away the shattered perspective of itself. The man, not wanting to exacerbate its pain by harping on the subject, thought it best to remain silent and let the creature console itself. Only those who have at one time or another been puffed up with the vainglories of their own beauty understand the dejection the moth suffered when it received the crushing blow of perception, not at the hands of the cruel world, but by those of the one dearest to it. The man returned to digging, while the creature bemoaned its fate.

Lying dormant in the valley of sorrow
A cocoon was found inside the moth
Strung tightly around the heart
It could not stop the bleeding

The following week, the creature remained aloof and refused to talk to the man. The old man did not seek to instigate any further harm, and surmised that when the creature was ready to talk, it would initiate conversation. Until then, at his regular slow but steady pace, the man continued digging. The creature did not know what to do. It sensed the man had told the truth, and, therefore, it should not be angry with him, but it was wroth and loathed the manner in which the man had so bluntly smashed its self-perception.

After wallowing for a time in self-pity, the creature decided it could not stay angry at the man, and whether a despicable creature or not, it did not have the capacity to hate anything for very long. So, as the man went about his work, the creature took to the adumbral sky of the pit and flew near him, seeking reconciliation.

The man recognized the creature signaling a token forgiveness, and, with such foresight, spoke the first words of truce to spare the despondent creature the trouble of formulating its own. "I am terribly sorry for how you took what I said, little creature, and I beg forgiveness for the blunt manner in which I went about it, but there is no easy way to dash the sense of self one creates. I fear I have destroyed your brittle ego, but in so doing have opened your eyes to the true vista of possibility."

The creature briskly forgave the man and told him it had come to terms with its fate. The man then told the creature that as awful as it seemed, the creature's fate was not so. From what he had seen of nature, the man believed moths to be misunderstood. Certain books of authority may have cited the moth as destructive and paired it with the locust, but that classification was simply a misunderstanding. The old man believed the moth to be a far more beautiful creature. He explained his belief to the somber creature that the moth could sense something, an elemental substance that entities emit. This was this reason it would cling to light, that it would sleep on windowsills to partake in the effluvium of humanity wafting through the window and warming its needy soul. The man went on to say, "It is simply probing light to gather the story of each place. Humans believe if walls could talk they would tell the story, but the truth is the light that emanates from us, from the sun and from the bulb, carries with it the story of time immemorial. It is the moth that has found the way to unravel the message such light carries. Some still think the moth is destructive, but it is rather the innate need to know the story that forces the moth to act, and anything that does not emit such light, like cloth, and fabric, is devoured as the moth seeks knowledge of the story."

The man turned to the creature, looked upon it as if he had discerned the entire life and fate of the poor thing, and said, "Sure, it will kill you to tell your story, little moth, but at least your life will serve a purpose. Butterflies do nothing but act beautiful; besides, outer beauty usually masks inner filth."

The man laughed, for his physical appearance possessed little, if any, of what the opposite sex might consider allure. The old man withdrew his chin from the wooden handle of the shovel, and began digging.

The creature, meanwhile, pondered the man's words, and realized he was right. There was some presence, an essence so real the creature could almost feel it exuding from the man, and it was that nebulous light that had drawn the creature to him, and it was that glow the creature had felt that warmed its entire being and kept it from leaving. The creature now realized in its first days of freedom it was drawn to those windowsills, against its will, because the attraction was too great to deny. The creature required such light to live. It fed off it. And the creature had discovered a supernal truth: The impulsion of a moth to seek out life-nurturing light is the same impulse of survival that guides a newborn's lips to a mother's nipple. And when the mouth receives the mother's milk, it does not question from where the nourishment flows; it simply knows it has been located. Neither does the moth need to fathom what the light is to enjoy its radiance. *So what*, thought the creature, *am I doing at the bottom of a pit? Why don't I flee and venture out into the light?* It feared the darkness more than anything, and, yet, for the creature, in the midst of the darkness, discerning the light was easiest, and it was here that the creature was unknowingly honing its skills.

IX

Over the next few weeks, the creature was unable to contain the excitement its abdomen harbored. It knew why it acted the way it did, and it recognized for the first time the immense import of what the man's digging quest could mean for the world. With fervent anticipation, it longed to tell the people what it and the old man had been doing. It also longed to discern and decipher the warmth and light emanating from humanity. From that moment on, every day was, for the creature, a burden. It wished the old man could dig a little faster and get a little deeper.

During this time, another type of transformation was affecting the creature. It did not know whether it was a natural metamorphosis that occurred to all moths or if it was caused in direct correlation with the old man's dashing its perception of self and helping it to recognize how to perceive the world, but the creature no longer saw the traits of old, wrinkly, and gray it had used to define the man. These characteristics were camouflaged by an actual emanation from the old man, and from the light that was the old man, the creature perceived moods, disappointments, emotions, and motives; however, this new power was just burgeoning and at times would flicker on, then off again. Only with time and repetition would the creature come to apprehend the relevance of its newfound power and be able to employ it. Regardless, this new revelation filled the creature with even more desire to leave the pit and venture into the world.

Daily, the creature would pine away in the old man's ear:

Should I fly up, yet, and tell the world what we have found? We are close, now, old man. I can sense it."

The man would look at the anxious creature and reply, "Patience, little creature. We are one-hundred feet deep at the most, the ground has grown hard, the pace is slow, and light or fire is nowhere near. We have just scratched the surface."

The old man's reply would not quell the creature's anxiousness. A moth's lifespan requires chronological events to proceed rapidly; otherwise, the moth feels as if it is wasting its short time. And measuring the creature's anxiety by human standards would be inadequate, for so short is the span of a moth's life and so valuable its last days that the moth cannot even find the time to eat. Humans do not experience an equivalent anxiety.

So, the creature would suffer attacks of restlessness, and it would count the minutes, the seconds, and wish it were time to flee the pit and tell the world the old man's story. It could not stand to watch another day pass without breaking through to the fire in the center, or hollowing out the earth and finding light on the other side. And, as the October sun descended and drew to a close another day at the bottom of the pit, the man sat his emaciated form upon the cold floor, curled up into a ball, pulled a blanket over his feeble body, and promptly went to sleep for the night.

As the man slept, the creature's anxiety increased. Later that night, it decided it must abandon the old man and take to the skies. The need to speak out was too pressing to stay at the bottom of the pit. The creature could not bear to wait any longer. It began its ascent. The pit had seemed so deep when from the bottom the creature used to look up at its mouth; the light had looked so distant. Now, as the creature was leaving, the nearness of the lip and each mark on the wall awoke a keen sense of just how little the old man had actually accomplished.

The winged creature cleared the rim and took one final look into the pit. At the heart of the immense darkness, it could just make out one, infinitesimal, white dot at the center of the black circle. The sleeping man resembled a distant and stellar pupil amid earth's dark iris.

At 2:25 a.m., the creature breathed in fresh air, and, as it made its way through the dark night and away from the pit, realized just how long the two had truly been digging. Although it may not have been a lengthy period of time when measured externally, internally it felt like an eternity. The creature shivered along, seeking some sort of light to rest its wearied head near. Clouds hid the moon's borrowed paleness. The night was pitch black.

WHEN STARS DIE

AFTER a restless night of wobbling back and forth in a
somnambulistic state, perched on a branch swarming with fireflies—the
only light it could find—the creature, groggy but feeling a vital energy
pulsing through its body for having made it to morning, took to the sky.
Rather than trying to pass over the formidable western mountains and
once more risk the nausea resulting from high altitude, and rather than
backtracking into the dark woods of its infancy and youth, it deemed it
best to attempt to cross the large, meandering river to see what verdant
pastures might lie beyond and what frolicsome humanity could be
dispersed eastward. It moved on, impassioned by its peculiar desire to
impart on humanity the message of the old man's struggle, to find light at
the heart of unnecessary suffering.

The creature had not flown long when it came across a crass-looking
man. The man's demeanor and appearance revealed all the customary
accoutrements of a vagabond: Unkempt clothing, an unruly air, unclean
skin, a miasmal stench, tarnished nubs for teeth, one silver and one gory-
colored orb for eyes, and, on top, a silly tuft of hair smack-dab in the
middle of his otherwise hairless pate that acted like a giant weathervane,
letting all know which way the wind blew, and, as an act of providence,
perhaps, letting all know which way to stand so as not to find themselves
downwind from him. Barring such blaring indicators of an invidious
disposition, the creature, attempting to discern light rather than judge
physical attributes, and desperately seeking the comfort of conversation,
assayed the man as suitable for such chatter.

What naiveté on the creature's part, for not only was the man
affected by a duality of personality that would cause him one moment to
sound refined, educated, even poetic, and the next philistine and vulgar,
emotions that came and went as randomly as the flipping of a coin, but a
human being would have noticed foremost the man's right eye's blind
pupil, gray as a fish scale, coated with mucus, and a human would have

shunned such a person. Clearly, the creature had not, as of yet, been indoctrinated into the world's standard of judgment, and, so, it fluttered near the man and, with childlike temerity, sought to capture his attention.

In full gait, the man noticed the creature, and, with a perspicuous glance upward, raised one side of his upper lip, creating a semi-scowl. Before the creature could retreat, which is what it wished to do after realizing the man's appearance might replicate his demeanor, the man perfunctorily asked: "What do you want, vermin?"

Unaccustomed to vituperative language, the creature remarked with meekness that it wished to cross the river, and wondered which route was best. The crass man told the creature he, too, was crossing, but rather than pay the toll and use the crowded ferry, he served as his own coxswain and captain in a tiny makeshift raft he had constructed from fallen timbers, and if the creature so desired, it could join him. "I just so happen to have one seat left for a creature of your size," mumbled the man.

His magnanimity of heart and joking nature offset the unkempt man's initial disagreeable demeanor, the demeanor, the creature now viewed, relied on as a simple ploy to keep people at a distance. Even so, the creature did not immediately respond to the man's generous offer. It had not decided on a proper course of action, and needed time to think. Naturally, it feared upsetting the man by being rude, but it also wanted to keep its options open, and, as of yet, the man omitted neither discernible light nor darkness. Worried that the silence had gone on too long and that not responding would be mistaken for a rejection, the creature told the unkempt man it was grateful for the offer, but would refrain from a decision until it could see the river.

Grumbling, the man protested, "Suit yourself, but I offered."

The unkempt man continued to converse with the creature by asking where it had come from and what it had been doing. In its zeal to express the singularity of the old man it had been assisting, the creature commenced a lengthy dissertation on its past few months. With alacrity, it explained how the old man was digging a hole in an effort to find light on the other side, or fire at the center. As the creature explained its enterprise, the man's gait slowed, and, in a brisk motion, his body raised and turned toward the creature as it described the old man.

Of a sudden, and in a peculiar manner, the coarse man stopped the creature mid-sentence with a jarring laugh accompanied by a halting wave of his hand. "Please stop. Please stop," the man begged with both his voice and hand, pleading as his midsection rumbled in convulsions. The man remained hunched over, and, each time he tried to compose himself, another fit of laughter afflicted him.

"You know him, I take it," said the creature, flummoxed, but wishing to understand what the man could possibly find so funny.

The unkempt man finally gathered his composure. He looked up at the creature, and, with a wry smile revealing his tar-stained teeth, stated: "Oh, yes, I believe I have made acquaintance with this man; this so-called 'digger of metaphysical holes.'" He explained to the creature that the old man had long been known around town as insane, as somewhat of a village idiot. "You mean to tell me, creature, you have been assisting the gravedigger's son? This was your venerable task?"

The creature did not respond to the man's derisive questioning. For that matter, the unkempt man did not expect the creature to say anything, for he sallied forth and continued to poke fun at an obvious sore spot.

After the man stopped having fun at the creature's expense by mocking the old man's method of digging holes, he told the creature of others who found the old man about as "smart as a sack of rocks," as he was fond of saying, those who had grown angry with the old man.

"Many a townsperson has sought redress after they happened to stumble upon and fall into one of the crazy man's abandoned and hazardous pits that pock the land and scarify an otherwise smooth surface. One such person is our town drunk. True, he is not the most trustworthy, but, no doubt, he did not fake the following incident, and, no doubt, the old man is at fault.

On this particular night, our town drunk could be found riveted to his usual seat at the end of the bar. And he could be found, as usual, rhythmically draining shots of heavy liquor into his stomach of steel and washing them down with a malt beverage. Well, when it came time for the saloon to close, the bartender sent the town drunk on his way to stumble through any open barn door he could find to curl up in the hay. Only, this moonless night, he so happened to be walking with an inebriated shuffle to his abode when he stumbled into one of the gravedigger's son's pits.

Falling into the abysmal black, he screamed out in despair: 'Hell hath enlarged herself and opened her mouth without measure, and I, unwittingly, have thrown myself into her gaping jowls.'

No sooner had he professed such drunken gibberish than he brutally bespattered the hole's bottom with his broken body. He lay there all night, cold and in agony. When the townsfolk found him the next morning, he lay unconscious. They did not think he would live. He had suffered two broken legs, a shattered pelvis, three cracked ribs, and to this day moans of incessant headaches and spells of dizziness. Fortunately, the only remedy for his malady was, and is, alcohol. However, this man does not find the digging of such pits laudatory, nor does he believe one might break through such a hard, cold crust and find light or life at the bottom, for he felt the brutal reality of that destitute, dark, and cold place when his body crashed into it, and he does not wish to ever encounter such a hole again."

The unkempt man continued, "If the tale were to end there, then, perhaps, the town drunk would not seek redress, but I have not shared the worst of it, creature. The poor man no longer feels safe stumbling through an open field or along the corridors of a dark alley. Because of his fall, he has set his parameters for life within the small town, and his time frame for living within the day. The man feels hedged in. Now, he only gets drunk when the sun is up. Can you fathom how degrading it is for this drunkard, this wild man who loves to roam the streets at night, to howl at the moon in inebriated moans; can you fathom what it costs him to be escorted, in the day, through an open barn door, and then laid down in the hay like a child? And all of this caused by your old man and his frenetic mind, which deemed it a good idea to burrow into the dirt. But, rest assured, vermin, the town drunk does think of your old man. Oh, yes. He dreams of bumping into the mentally-deranged gravedigger's son, so he can usher in a period of bruised darkness for him as well. Unfortunately, such a meeting has not as yet transpired, but, if the town drunk ever, or many others who share his sentiments, come across your venerable old man, they would greet him with a lot more than a smile, if you know what I mean. That loose dirt and empty pit would be put to good use."

The unkempt man laughed and then checked himself before he embarked on another fit of hysterics. The creature did not like to hear such rubbish spoken about the old man, and it would not allow the man to continue to jeer and mock any longer. The creature pleaded for the man to stop.

The unkempt man turned to the creature with hatred spilling from his different-colored eyes, and said, "Why should I not speak of him in such a manner? He is my older brother, after all. I am the one who bears, on his behalf, the brunt of the townspeople's jokes."

This revelation stunned the creature. It could not find the words to speak, but its selection would not have mattered anyway. The man ceased having fun at the creature's expense, having arrived at the banks of the river.

In the distance, the ferry sounded but could not be seen. The creature recognized the outline of a throng of workers lined up, awaiting its arrival. A sliver of fog clung to the river's surface, and, as the crowning sun gleamed through the fog, shrouded the river in ghostly white. The man stumbled down the steep banks and called to the creature, inviting it to join him once more. The river was wide and the creature's wings were not tested for such a long journey. The creature looked once more at the distant crowd it had wished to join, and realized the tight quarters of the ferry and the crowd itself filled it with apprehension. The creature decided, as unruly as the man behaved, it had better join him. The man shoved off from the shore and became a shadow as the mist swallowed his boat. The creature flew into the brume and alighted on the far end of the makeshift raft so as to face the man.

Once it lost sight of the shore, deep melancholy overcame the creature. It held fond memories of the place it had just left, and wondered whether it was making the right decision by venturing out. Since abandoning the old man and the pit, the creature's mind had remained fixed on exploring new areas, laying eyes on violent horizons, mingling with foreign people, and imparting its knowledge, but as the boat scurried deeper into the clouded unknown, doubt enshrouded the little creature, and it began to question its course of action. Perhaps the eerie feeling was a consequence of its current surroundings. For, it was true the mist seemed to create an unreal atmosphere, accentuating and exacerbating the ghastly features of the man captaining the tiny raft. The thought of returning to shore entered the creature's mind, but the fear of losing its way in the thick obscurity of mist served as a successful impediment. The creature consigned itself to kismet, enduring the remainder of the crossing with the unkempt man.

The creature looked at the man and noticed a drastic change occurring within, or upon, him. The man's features, already distorted due to his impairments, waxed stronger in their ghastliness, and what had appeared human took on a demonic countenance in the impervious mist. This phenomenon was caused by nothing more than the sun disappearing behind a cloud, but the creature couldn't fathom this, and, gullible to the fantastic as the innocent sometimes are, it believed the masked vagabond a ruse a cover for the Moloch now arising. The man's ploy seemed simple enough: Get the creature to tag along until no one could see the transformation and devouring.

Precisely at this point, the demon released a nefarious laugh from deep within its gut, sending a shiver down the creature's very abdomen. "You grow scared, creature. I perceive it." The man's gory eye flashed at the little creature. He lifted the long pole he had been using as an oar and switched sides, then dipped it back into the murky water.

The sun reappeared, and the shadows distorting the man's features fled, marking the reappearance of the simple vagabond. The creature began to relax, realizing its blunder, but the man's stare remained fixed. The creature shifted to avoid the seeing eye, but the man would not relinquish. Finally, with his good eye still fixed upon the creature, the man pointed to himself with his index finger, and, lightly tapping his breast, said, "Do not fear me, little one, nor let my outward aspect frighten you. I understand you, do I not? I speak to you, and when you speak to me, I hear what you say, do I not? It is those you will meet on the other side whom you should fear, creature. Sure, they may look normal, but they will not be able to understand you. They lack the capacity to discern the susurrations of your imperceptible heart."

The man's voice remained on even keel except for the slight inflection each time he said "I," or "me," or "they"—words he accompanied with a heftier pounding of his index finger to his breast. The unkempt man, beginning to reveal his double nature, a nature which, once betrayed, rarely floundered back to acquiescence, but rather ran its course then fizzled out, began semi-pleading with the creature:

"You should turn back before it is too late. You embark upon a hopeless journey; I fear it will end badly." Then, the man's mood shifted, and he spoke happily. "But why all this negative talk, huh? You should be hallowed by a good omen from me; not a bad omen."

The man's mood vacillated again. With ferocious strokes of his open palm, the man began hitting himself on the forehead and repeating, "What is a good omen? What is a good omen?"

The creature watched the man's hem and haw actions and listened to his speech not knowing quite what to do or make of the strange vagabond that seemed to be possessed by archfiends both offensive and non-provocative.

With abruptness, the unkempt man ceased striking himself and raised his head toward the creature with a new and sinister sparkle in his bloodshot eye. The man beseeched the creature to leave the stern and advance toward him. "Come closer, fly. There is something I must give you."

The creature did not dare budge. It was alarmed by the man's erratic behavior. And, the disarming quality of the man's voice seemed baiting. It sounded the way a little boy might sugarcoat his pleading when he holds out a piece of meat to a dog he wishes to ensnare the second it gets nears enough.

"Come closer, creature. I wish to bless you before you embark."

The creature still did not move. It sensed something off kilter in the man's beseeching, and the mist debilitated the creature's ability to discern light. Light or no light, it wanted to trust him, and, until this point, besides being moody, the man had done nothing to dissuade the creature from believing he would not behave according to his word. Rather than fly into some sort of trap, the creature questioned the man from where it perched. "What might you bless me with?"

"That I will not tell you. I only assure you that it might save you from the myriad sufferings you will face upon your journey. If you come closer—simpleton that I am—I assure you, I will impart an invaluable gift. A gift any traveler commencing their journey into the unknown would be jealous of and require. Even my brother, your friend, would approve of this gift."

The honeysuckled words produced the unkempt man's desired effect. The too-trusting creature suffered itself to be ensnared by the man's offer. "Okay, I will accept your gift, but promise me this is not some sort of trap."

The man told the creature what it wanted to hear. The creature flew toward the man, and landed before him. "What is it you have to offer?"

The man scratched his stomach and then looked down at the creature. "Ah, yes, my offering." The man turned and pretended to grab something from inside his tattered jacket. In truth, the unkempt man turned so he could dredge up as much phlegm and spittle as he could muster from his tracheal regions. He turned to the creature, fully loaded, and extended his cupped hand as if offering the alms. "Here is the gift," gurgled the man, with his mouth full and closed.

As the unsuspecting creature drew near, the vagabond waited for the perfect moment, and, when it came, expectorated the entire mouthful of spit toward the creature. The spittle flew at the creature, ominous and dark as it approached, momentarily blocking the sun. The viscous glob's gravity forced it to stretch thin in the middle, with a discus hurling at each end like a twirling baton. As the descent of a carnivorous raven circling inert carrion, the slow-moving glob, spinning end over end, made its way to, and hit, the awed creature. The initial blow inundated the creature and sent it sprawling backwards across the deck. It landed sideways, completely drenched in the mucilaginous film. Stunned both by the velocity of the strike and the audacity of the man's action, the creature could not move. The man's nefarious laughter returned with vigor, and, in a sacrilegious gesture, the unkempt man crossed himself before spouting off, "I baptize you! By the authority of this Earth, I baptize you!"

The man remained hunched over the creature, laughing, with spit drizzling from the corners of his mouth, his offensive archfiend nature in total control. The fit of hysterics passed, and the man raised himself to full length, scratched his belly, and then performed a cabalistic, pagan-looking dance, accompanied by a chant:

"Ashes to ashes. Dust to dust. Best start out filthy. For in God we rust."

The unkempt man shuffled his feet from side to side, and, each time he said "rust," he lowered his entire body near the planks of timber and pointed at a carving of two sheaves of wheat bound with coiled grapevines. The intertwined wheat and grapevine, toward the base, transformed into two snakes. The natural inclination of the eye drifted to the snakes' jaws, dislocated and gaping, revealing venomous teeth—like each was about to attempt to swallow the other. The curvature of the snakes' bodies formed a disconnected heart that almost touched at the connecting point of the two gaping mouths. Impressed upon the dazed creature and pirouetting through its mind at heart-rate speed spun the peculiar thought that the carving was not there when the two embarked upon the journey. *The man must have been standing upon it, hiding it,* thought the creature.

After reveling in his vulgar behavior, the man turned to the creature, stopped dancing, stood upon the carving to hide it once more, and with the sternest of looks, stated: "I have baptized you in the foul water of this earth, little creature. Now—now—you are ready to embark upon your journey. I have christened you with the filth of a world run amok. Only now, creature, will you be able to face the angry, crude, and miserable world and not dry heave, not vomit back in its inanimate face. This christening is a gift of inestimable value. I hope you recognize its worth. "

The man concluded his words, and then bowed his head in affected reverence.

The creature did not move. Its wings were sticky and the dust that kept them dry remained coated in viscous spit. The creature kept trying to flap its wings to flip off the spittle, but the process was slow going. It did not straightway ascend out of the waters of its baptism, so to speak. It took time and a monotonous effort of flinging spit off its wings before the creature dried enough to fly. And, as quickly as it could, it did. It landed on the outermost edge of the tiny raft's stern. The creature sat with its wings extended, revealing two dark patterned eyes, and let the sun conclude the drying process. The unkempt man disgusted the creature. It felt his dirty spit clinging to its body, and, even where it was dry, it still could feel a film.

From the bow of the ship, the man, still in a hypnotic, almost Dionysian state, began hollering at the creature, cupping his hands near his mouth as if he were speaking to a large audience or over a great divide that required his voice to carry: "Speechless, I see. They say spiritual experiences are hard to convey, and I expect such is the case with you. Well, rest assured, creature, I won't ask you to share your sacred experience. Keep it all to yourself and ponder its significance. Such is the only way to understand mysterious things."

Scratching his belly, then returning his hands to a cupped position, the man prattled on: "One final word of advice. As your spiritual advisor, I feel it necessary to counsel you not to take forty days to ponder the significance of your baptism—you won't live that long."

His final comment sent the unkempt man into another fit of hysterics that started off slowly with a single "ha," but ended in a steady stream of "hahahas."

Watching the man convulse in guffawed spasms, the creature wished, once more, not as a nostalgic aching, but an honest desire, to be in the company of the old man whose side it had left. *These two men, polar opposites, could not be kin*, thought the creature.

Maintaining his gaze upon the creature, which shifted and shuddered under such a glowering look, the man fell silent as the offensive archfiend began its retreat into the dark recesses of his mind. Then, the unkempt man sat down and began contemplating, or reminiscing. His gored eye grew distant, his mood somber; an improved, inoffensive archfiend commenced its arrival. As quickly as he had fallen into a trance, he snapped out of it and looked at the creature, enthralled by some new thought. "You know..." he began, with exhilaration in his voice. "You know, creature, a heart is a curious thing. Those who come into the world with it shattered can do one thing: Reconstruct. They can fill the void. And, they can mend the broken heart with the binding glue of experience and brotherhood. They can do so because they are young and do not have anything against which to compare their broken heart. I have always felt sorrier for the man who loses his sight in an accident than the one born into blindness. The one who loses sight later in life remembers what vision impinged upon his memory, his psyche, or he remembers the bliss of a green hillside, but the one born with the handicap has nothing against which to compare blindness, and, therefore, cannot wallow in self-pity nor note the discrepancies between vision and sightlessness. And, the same can be said of the heart. Those who come into the world with a heart full of love, a heart taught to strain and reach for some unobtainable ideal, inevitably will witness it shattered, and with the fractured pieces the ideal is swept away."

The man did not just mutter these words with icy indifference. His voice was imploring and full of animation. His motions were eccentric and wrought with contortions, and, his hands, like a painter trying to scour the canvassed sky with a rainbow, flew up and over his body.

He continued. "On the one hand, the heartbroken at birth construct something positive from the realism they are confronted with because, at an early age, realism is all they know. In opposition, those whose hopes are dashed after the ideals are firmly set in their minds have the hardest time dealing with harsh reality. They try to keep their heads in the lofty clouds of their ideals, but with every step they feel the rug of failed hope yanked out from under their feet. They are so enamored with the ideal and perfection that cannot be obtained that they refuse to let it go. At the same time, they grow disgusted with cruel reality that is far below, and, oftentimes the destroyer of, the ideal they have imagined. Because of the incongruous nature of real life versus ideal life, they refuse to use reality as a stepping stone to obtain their ideals, and, so, they, of all people, remain the farthest from their ideals and become a nuisance to those functioning in the real world."

The man's abnormal motions slowed. His hands expressed solemnity; they were no longer painting rainbows in the canvassed sky. He interlocked his fingers like four pairs of motionless wings, while his thumbs, two wriggling worms, essed in place upon his sternum.

He kept excoriating the poor creature—albeit the creature hadn't the slightest clue that the man's purpose suggested anything other than babble. "They are hopeless dreamers, chanting to themselves: 'Between the idea and the reality, between the motion and the act, falls the shadow.' It's always the shadow with this type. For them, life is a drawn-out affair lived beneath an imperfect sun whose rays bluff the truth they withhold, all the while casting impregnable shadows upon the entire scene. I'd be willing to wager, creature, if you could probe the heart of history—more specifically, if you could probe the hearts of the believers in the ideal world to come and the hearts of those who are disbelieving of such nonsense, I bet you would discover the firmest of believers originated as the gravest of doubters, and the gravest of doubters originated as the firmest of believers. Would you take me up on such a wager?"

The creature remained silent, refusing to answer the unkempt man.

"Of course you wouldn't, you neophyte. You still cling to your own distorted ideals," the man said, pestering the creature, before carrying on.

"If one could skip through time and walk alongside the most infamous of all traitors, my hypotheses is they would find one who early on in life was, if not completely converted, at least one of the first disciples, and probably one of the first to embrace wholeheartedly and adhere to the ideals taught him. He would have been an idealist at first, and, only over time, when the flesh did not measure up to his ideal, would he have turned so bitter. Bitter enough to complete the dastardly deed of betrayal with a kiss. A kiss—the most intimate of symbols for the flesh. The poet has penned, 'It is heaven's hammer in hallowed hands which strikes a hole in the heart of man deeper than hell could ever hollow.' But, we can never know what specific gall wormed its way into this traitor's heart. Only this do we know about human nature: It was, and still is, and always will be, true—the heart loves, at first, to oppose anything one holds dear. The heart is the first to grow disillusioned with the ideals it has so strongly accepted. You see, creature, it would have been better for this traitor to have lived like the obstinate disbeliever from the Book of Acts. Set out on the wrong path and your opposing heart will lead you to the right one. But, if you start on the right path—trust me, your heart will lead you astray."

The man remained entranced by what he was saying. Even his thumbs ceased their wriggling. Never before had he enjoyed an audience, which emboldened him. "It is the same with love, creature. If you want a woman to love you, hate her dearly, and, over time, you will come to love the object of your loathing, and she will come to love you, but if you start out in love, trust me, she will sense helplessness and her heart will react with opposing, brutal force—it will love to hate you; it will loathe your love; it will spitefully use and ultimately destroy you, and, over time, your heart will also grow to hate her. Ah, the workings of man's tragic heart. Compared to it, there is nothing."

The man said no more on the subject. Even a gracious audience of one could not prolong the inevitable ending—he was spent. So, too, was his inoffensive archfiend. It disappeared into the same dark recesses as the first.

The creature disregarded what the man said, although it could not help but sympathize with him. The creature could discern something had wilted the verdant life within the man's breast, and the shell the creature now gazed upon was the simple result of a life no longer able to struggle against vicissitudes. *When the light of life leaves the body it once possessed,* thought the errant creature, *darkness fills the cavity, and it would have been better for that body to have never known such light.* Unfortunately, life does not, like the last line of a fable, offer itself up to such a didactic summary, and, more often than not, light and darkness, though they cannot conjoin, coexist and grow together like the wheat with the tares, and only with the reaping of the harvest can it be known what truly has been sown in one's heart.

The raft drifted onward, the unkempt man no longer steering. The creature hoped the current would not lead them astray. The man sat with his knees bent and his head fallow between his thighs. The creature felt a strange compassion for its offender, but was reluctant to turn the feeling into action; the man's grief extended beyond its scope of sympathy. The man continued to wallow in his misery. Old wounds were the only semblance of a life he had from which to cling. Sometimes, there are those macabre souls who seem destined to cherish their misery because it is the last emotion that reminds them they once lived. Sometimes, in life, there are even those who seek out such misery, but this man was not one of them—misery sought him out. The creature could sense it. More like misery chose the man as a vessel to carry, and, when necessary, disseminate its virile seed. The creature could also sense that whatever the man suffered was a tailored type of suffering whose affliction had been designed specifically for him because it was the only agony the man could not handle. Almost as if misery catered itself uniquely to each body. As if, as a parasite, it has learned to present itself in a manner fitting entrance of a door that would otherwise remain shut. With its subtle knock and beguiling countenance, it manages to persuade the occupant to turn the knob. Once inside, the true destruction begins, a destruction specific to a host lacking immunity.

The man raised his head and began inaudibly mumbling. As the creature grew accustomed to the soft mutterings, it began to decipher the words. In a voice rife with melancholy, the unkempt man regurgitated the same two verses:

> There was a time when meadow, grove, and stream,
> The earth and every common sight,
> To me did seem
> Apparell'd in celestial light,
> The glory and the freshness of a dream.

> Now each time I pass a meadow, grove, or stream,
> The earth and every common blight,
> To me doth seem
> Apparell'd in devilish fright,
> The horror and the madness of a scream.

After numerous recitations, for good measure the man reiterated a portion of his last line: "The madness of a scream, I say!"

And then, he ceased repeating himself. The creature stiffened and refused to allow the wind to stir a wing. The man's gory eye burned red, and his blind eye glistened like a silver coin, presenting a frightening image of sincere bestiality. Then, the eye softened and his posture relaxed. He moved as if he prepared to enact something sententious, which he did.

He started hitting his breast again, this time with solid *thwacks* from his closed fist, and, in dulcet tones, which were incongruous to the subject at hand, raved on poetically insane: "What good is a heart? The amaranthine pendulant caged within the matrix of bone. Beat on, you glorified pump. Drum your toxic plasma through this tenement of flesh. Pump on, you hemoglobin. Animate this tabernacle of napping clay. Ah, the human heart, the anathema of the mortal experience. If I could sunder the breastbone, bury my hands in the chasm, and wrench the heart out yet beating, I would—I would. I would toss it on terra firma, trample it underfoot, and then feed it to salivating dogs. But all would be for naught. The cursed thing does not die. Locked inside, it continues its aching beat; over and over, I feel its incessant drumming. Would some merciful god strike it down and nullify its existence, erase its pain and fill it with blank darkness, pure absence of light, then, and only then, will I live. Why, oh, why, did you ever teach me to love, cursèd heart?"

By the time the unkempt man had concluded his diatribe and lay splayed across the raft, extremities groping toward the poles, his face and bloated belly heavenward, the raft continued to drift toward its unknown destination. The intermittent growling of the man's stomach ruptured the muteness. At first, both creature and human chose to ignore the grumblings. But when the sound grew too loud, the man sat up, patted his belly, and explained to the creature how, like clockwork, his stomach was telling him it was time for lunch. "Hush, now," said the man, while soothing his belly. "All we have to eat is this vermin with wings, and I know how you detest the taste of vermin."

The creature remained resolute in its refusal to speak another word to the man who had maliciously spit upon it, and, so, even in danger of being eaten, it stayed silent.

"Lighten up, would you? I wouldn't really eat you. Your wings would just get caught in my gullet."

The unkempt man was too tired to guffaw. He chuckled once, and another silence ensued. The raft continued to drift.

Then the man sat up, grabbed his pole of an oar, and looked back toward the creature. "I know, creature, you must be thinking: 'This is not a river; this is an ocean.' Well, we have reached the other side, and our time to part has come."

And, as the man said these last words, the raft slithered up the muddy bank. The creature was relieved the time had come to part from such a tragic, disagreeable man. The man jumped off the raft, and, grabbing the rope tied to the front, wrapped it around a lone, dead tree trunk. The creature fluttered upward, on the verge of leaving the calloused man without saying a word, but, before it could fly off, the man spoke. "Creature," he said, not parting his teeth to speak. The wind of words came out like jetted venom, and the creature knew it did not want to hear what the man would say next, but it felt trapped by a skewed sense of propriety. It felt that it must listen to the man because he had shuttled it across the river. "Creature," the man continued in the same manner, "one more thing, before you leave."

The man stepped up the undercut bank so as to stand level with the fluttering creature. Reaching its height, the man's one gory and one gray-blotted eye looked directly at the creature as he continued: "If you go, you will not again cross this river alive. Mark my words." His perturbed voice rose in fury. "So, before your short life is spent, weigh the costs. You will long, like never before, for the place you have left, yet, you will not make it back alive." The man had reached the angry apogee of his harangue, and when his voice should have been loudest, it grew calm and admonishing, and his bleared eye looked strained and tired, like his next words were tearing up his insides. He whispered in earnest supplication, "Why not turn back now? Why not turn back before it is too late, creature?"

The creature was touched by the man's importuning and wondered whether his point was not valid, but the innate longing to speak to the world had carved a cavity of longing in the creature too long, and to turn back before telling people about the old man's digging, or to relate how close he was to finding light at the bottom of that dank, dark pit, would be like trying to stop a wheel, hurtling downhill, from spinning. Also, the desire to do the opposite of what the vagabond suggested burned within—in a sense, doing so, the creature considered its strange baptism repudiated. The creature did not respond to the man's importuning, but started to flutter away.

Frustrated with the irresponsive creature, the man broke off his calm speech and reverted to his vituperative tone. "Your journey is pointless, creature, and will only end in failure." He yelled at the top of his lungs, fists raised in the air. "You do the bidding of a raving lunatic. The gravedigger's son, my older brother, is deranged, and will not find in all his digging anything worthwhile." The man spat out his barbed words with rapaciousness. "I'll tell you what he will find at the bottom of all that dirt, creature—more dirt. More cold, hard, crusted, indifferent dirt. Nothing else. And, I will tell you what you will find on this side of the river, creature—more people. More cold, hardened, crusted, indifferent people."

The man prattled on, but the creature had had enough and flew higher as quickly as possible, its wings beating like the thumbing of pages through a large book, and away it went. But the unkempt man's final words were carried on the more speedy wind, and the spear-like shaft of such venom-drenched words spitted the poor creature's very soul. And, like a mortally wounded animal pays special attention to the voracious howl of the pack of wolves fast approaching, knowing each drop of its leaking blood has communicated its scent of vulnerability, so, too, were the creature's ears perked to know what rapidly closed in on it. And the man's last words: "You will die alone! You will die brokenhearted!" wounded the creature beyond description. It knew behind his mad howl existed dark truth.

II

The creature cleared a line of trees adjacent to the river, averting the man's incessant cries from piercing its ears. It could perceive a small city in the distance. The city was dotted with rustic buildings, dilapidated tenements, and all kinds of shops. The usual cacophony of city sounds— the whistling of trains and screeching of cars—resounded. The creature needed to rest. It had grown tired, and the poignancy of the unkempt man's actions and remarks weighed upon its dreary soul. Near the city's edge, the creature came upon a small clearing covered in wilted yellow-brown grass. On the far side of the park sat a lone woman on a bench. The creature at once encountered amazement at the innate pathos such a picturesque, crestfallen, dejected-looking woman could stir. On the river's other side it had never stumbled upon a woman exhibiting such queenly grace, let alone one with the visage of a cracked crown, a depressing weight bearing down and around her that could not detract from her glory. No sooner had it spotted her than all thought of its own pain, and the horrible sting from the vagabond's final words vanished like the dew beneath a scorching sun.

What a sight of tragic beauty. The contrast of the woman's vibrant red hair against her lifeless, pale skin was like the shrill cry of a newborn in a funeral procession. The creature left the periphery and headed toward the woman, before realizing its mistake. Her pale skin was not deceased, just pellucid, and, underneath its transparency, the blue veins of translucent life flowed so near the surface that the creature watched its pulse gush like a river. The brittleness of a butterfly wing, a thin layer of ice, a cracking leaf underneath a foot, was evinced from a single glance at the thin covering of skin, and at the nucleus of the woman's genteel fragility sat two eyes that bespoke an ancient hurt.

Her eyes penetrated not with force or malice, but rather like an eddy that throughout a river's existence has gathered every piece of debris fallen into the river, and, once the eddy has spun around for a time, sends on its way. Her eyes, too, had gathered a lifetime's detritus of suffering. The eyes were serene, but, beneath their surface imperturbation, a sunken, silent pain yet roiled.

Hypnotized by stubborn beauty's gravitational pull, the creature scarcely noticed the woman before it reeled in a direct path toward her face, caught in the current of attraction's fustian pulse. On the creature, time loosened its grip, and magnificent beauty reeled it in: Head-first.

The creature watched the woman's grief adulterate the dim surrounding light. The creature flew into the sullied stream in an attempt to ascertain the woman's story. For all her obliviousness, however, the woman noticed the creature hovering, and, in an effortless swoop of her arm, collected the creature the way a hen gathers a chick under its wing at the first sign of imminent danger, and cradled it in the cavern of her fist. She then placed it on her lap. The creature knew by her arm's gentle movement, and by the feathered softness of her hand's doting and infallible grip, no present danger existed. It looked up at the woman and reveled in the entrancement of her gaze.

Staring into those eyes, the creature discerned a voice as soft as velvet ask in susurrations, "What are you doing disturbing my time of quiet reflection?"

The voice sounded so supple the creature believed it had not been heard, but felt. The creature attempted to deliver its usual acquiescent reply, but, instead of effable tones, made out the rattle of some foreign sound. Perplexed, it attempted again to speak. And, although the vowels and consonants formed syllables inside its head, and although the image of what it would say appeared tangible, when it set those words like hot coals upon its tongue and sought to spew them into the air, they came out sounding like the gut-wrenching metallic noise of grinding gears. So harsh spewed forth the sound that the creature immediately fell silent.

The woman continued to cast her entrancing stare upon the creature, and, then, suddenly, allowed her widening gaze to take in the entire panorama. Her eyes grew distant as she stared at a copse of trees at the park's far end. "Well," said the velveteen voice, "since you won't speak to me, I will tell you my story. It will be nice to share it with a creature lacking the capacity to retell."

The creature heard the woman's words, but never saw her mouth move, and, for the first time, realized the woman spoke not at all, but in the soft-lighted essence clinging to her, the light gathering around her unspooled itself slowly, relating the tale of her sad life. Constant coils of amber light spoke of recollections on the theme of love:

What a day. What a lovely day. Him, here at my side, and, each time my hand touches his, it sends myriad sparks through the endless highways of membranous tubes converging within the chamber of my systolic heart, then, in diastoles knowing no bounds, the sparks, in metered rhythm, spread outward to the nethermost reaches of a body: A body of both space and eternity: How does blood know what to feel? It is blood, not brain, that speaks to the poet, supplies him phrases rife with meaning. I require a poet's tongue, or at least a poet's hand. A poet could explain how time, space, and eternity are encapsulated in two single pulses—could define it, give it a name, put it down in writing: Could explain how each touch is a veritable lifeline of electricity flowing through my arteries and reaching the hub of my being; becoming more real, more dependable than any ant army's marching columns; becoming more instinctual, more on cue, more perfect than the hexagonal honey cells of the bee's hive; becoming Nature's greatest feat—the incarnation of love.

The poet could explain how with every rush of ecstasy caused by a single touch—a covering of flesh comes in contact with another piece of flesh—and each taut squeeze—flesh prickled and a vague sense of the warmth and bone underneath— raises the notes of love to a celestial chord; a chord unimaginable. Is there no wall, no barrier, to such love? Is the inside of man like a parcel of land, the canopied flesh a useless fence and the sempiternal sky one's ever-growing emotions? Emotions One brushes against, but never stops to fathom just how far they reach. Is the body holding One back, keeping One from exploring the heights of true affection? If so, the body is nothing, and emotion came first, rose up out of time immemorial and clothed itself in flesh. It must be love, curtained itself with flesh, so it can experience touch. Yes, the body was a means—a means to express love, but somehow the experiment has gone awry, forgotten in birth, or, if not forgotten, then suppressed— or even more than suppressed—emotion itself is trapped inside this machine of sinew, cartilage, and matter. And, trapped underneath the labyrinth of flesh, vein, and bone, these emotions remain beyond expression and caged, forever struggling to escape. Nature's greatest blunder—the incarnation of love.

If I spoke with the poet's tongue, I could bring these emotions back to the surface, could paint the fugacious face of love. Love is like the opera singer's songs whose notes you think cannot possibly climb higher, but, when they do, you believe they have reached the utmost constraints of vocal capacity; they will not climb the ladder to grasp a higher note, but then they climb one note higher, rung by rung, and the pitch verges on the unreal, and the crescendo process of climbing the scale continues; each time you set a limit for what the timbre of the voice can reach, the singer defies it and on their voice rises, and then you wonder when that voice will reach such a celestial pitch that it surpasses the human ear's ability to hear; when that voice, so angelic, will begin breaking glass; when it will reveal its true purpose and turn destructive? And then you wonder, as he again squeezes your hand, when does the emotion surpass the body's capability to contain it? When does emotion become so powerful it destroys the flesh that confines it? Then, you start to measure and weigh the consequences of touch, and you realize the danger of giving in to emotion. Then, you think to yourself, I must chain my heart of fleshy glass, not let it escape the bounds of my body; I must construct a wall around my heart; the pitch is verging on destruction—the heart, or rather, the love within, is seeking escape. I must house my heart within the confines of human capacity—too much love is the sin that will kill quicker than all the hate the world holds. And, yet, I fear I have reached an emotional tone, hit a note already incomprehensible. Why do I feel this way around him? When will such a note destroy one of us?

No wonder the romantic poet dies young. He was meant to, before love evaporates or abscesses, before the world stops rhyming, or before love sounds out of tune, so that all he knows is the limitless note of love spanning the sidereal, and, by his own dissolution, he forfeits incarnate life but rejoins the love he was torn from in mortality. Is this what I want for myself? No, I want a realist's tongue, not a poet's, and I want love to remain in the flesh. And, after it has come to fruition, only then does love limp into the eternal, does it rear up after death, does it light the way through galaxies of darkness—then, and only then, after the incarnate thing has returned to spirit form, is it worthy of its name.

The discarded light revealed the woman's innermost thoughts, simple corollaries in the throes of love, but then it skipped over thin reels of time and started to unravel a different thread of the woman's story, revealing sadder moments locked within her brittle heart.

The dejected woman's stare fixed upon a single blade of grass that lay before her:

It was here. On this very spot that Time's incessant ticking ceased and eternity drooped her cosmic cape that caught me in her infinite sag. I cannot move forward or backward. I am stuck replaying the same scene over and again. We were walking here. Hand in hand, our conjoined fingers functioned as an umbilicus— making us one and administering to love's sustenance. What a day, creature. Life only affords us so much time with both the ferocity and immensity of feeling, and, yet, within the overload of feeling, a total ataraxia takes hold. During those days, a person becomes one with the universe, with the amoral substance supporting all life. How could the person not know the moment is in transit, is dying at the very time it is burgeoning, is a life and death in itself—for all moments scraping against eternity and wishing not to be confined within the realm of time and space are ultimately quashed by a beckoning return to the inimical laws of this time-trapped earth. Such laws bring solace to the sufferer whose pain is but for a moment and then gone, but they also ferry sorrow to the infatuated, for, try as they might, they cannot relive the first fleeting moments of love.

But what of those who are trapped in the cold basin of eternity, those who live their extrinsic and mortal lives in the field of time, but their intrinsic and eternal emotions in the field of repetitive everlastingness? For, there are such souls. Must we not try to think of such things? Must we tarry on content with our allotted avenues of release from such thought? For, if some are more in tune with the eternity functioning within them, they lose sight of this world's glamour, and this world loses its hold on them, and then these people wander into a no-man's land, caught between time and eternity, always longing for what this life cannot grant—love unbound from flesh.

I should have known I was in trouble the first time his hand touched mine. Love was surreal, too good to be true and too true to be bound, and I knew it. I felt the premonition as tangibly as if it were whispered: 'Too much love will destroy you.' I should have heeded the warning and constructed a wall around my heart, but I was stubborn. I floated upon the ethereal wings of love, but, oh, how the plunge from such a height racks my soul. Flying too near the sun—that was my mistake—burnt these butterfly wings! Over and over, I watch myself plummet from sidereal heights. Time and again, I watch as those wings are consumed by fire. How could I not have known? How could I have been so brazen to think I could get away with a love unfit for this world? Never could an imperfect world permit a perfect love.

We are but wanderers, sojourners in a land unfit to call home, inhabitants of a body lent from mortality, wandering through an infinite night on the invisible sun, knowing least of all our motives and ourselves.

But, enough of this wallowing in the mire of self-pity. I must move on, must recover from the shattered moments, must form a new me from the ashes, yet self-reproach is all I have left! To deny me my self-reproach, to deny me the constant sorrow, the pity, would eradicate the validity of the moment that brought me here. I do wish to shed forth a different light, but how? I am stuck creating new versions of the same story. It is the only story I know. It is the only story that matters. The old heartache will not, for one minute, leave me. It is there when I wake, like a boulder on my chest, and it is my final thought before sleep. Most nights, it haunts my dreams. Try as I might, there is no escaping this story. I cast new characters, create new backdrops, but the theme will never change. Over and again, the same events occur:

Here, we were walking in unison. Right here, on this very spot of grass, our feet trod on these very blades. We did not know where we were going, nor did we care—love is directionless. We only knew we were together, and, if the world and its inhabitants disappeared, what did it matter? We had each other. This is what I was thinking as we walked in this park. Then, off in the distance, I heard a loud crack or bang and a simultaneous whizzing sound like a lead wasp destroying the very air it usurped. I heard the unearthly shattering, cringing noise of lead smashing against bone and flesh. What a ghastly sound! No ocean, swelling to colossal proportions and bashing its unruly fist upon any fissure or cleft of rock, no melon dropped from astronomical heights and smashing its pulpous guts upon the earth's hardened crust, not even a planet colliding with another, none of these sounds could match the unearthly peal of the rapid-fired lead smashing into the skull; that ossified crack, that lead stinger entering the soft brain tissue, then metal exiting bone, and the trailing firebrand of the man's spewing essence, giant red spurts mixed with skull shrapnel, spackled the afternoon with its surreal nebulous of blood.

Oh, creature, instantaneously his umbilical hand, the source of so much electricity, so much life, went limp. Light fled; in broad daylight, midnight's rapture poured upon me. His body, the weight of a millstone wrapped around his neck, became gravity's latest victim, and pulled me down as I held onto his lifeless hand. We crashed atop this very spot. His ravaged head bled right here. I point in front of me, but I no longer see the blood. I look at the grass where he once lay, but the human stain does not remain on a single blade of this year's resurrected and now-dying grass. No, creature, the grass has moved on, has lived another life, died, and lived again. All things have progressed, but I cannot. I know he bled out his life right here, in front of where I now sit, where I was snubbed of the only thing that matters in life. How, tell me how, creature, could one move on? The shock of such a moment renders one numb, petrified, a pallid shell of our former self.

By the time our bodies slammed to the ground, I knew he was dead and there was no resuscitating him, no bringing him back to this life. So, I did the only thing I could, creature. I took his head, placed it in my lap, and cradled it as the blood gurgled then spurted out and puddled in the dimpled part of my dress. The puddle of blood saturated the fabric and dripped back to earth to rejoin the soil from which we humans long ago sprang. And I sat, cradling his head, rocking back and forth, thinking to myself: 'Oh, anemic man, whose life is in his nostrils. Is this all it takes to wipe out an entire being? A breathing, walking, thinking entity can be annihilated in the matter of a moment? One measly piece of lead can destroy something thirty years in the making? Not thirty years in the making; thirty years in the flesh. Flesh that required the sun to shine to come into being, the globe to orbit at just the right distance, one-celled life to emerge from the sea and evolve, and on it has gone since time immemorial—an infinite number of circumstances needing to be just right in order for this one life to come into being, grow, and progress to the age of thirty. And it was all for naught. Life, you falsifier of hopes! You raise us so high one moment, only so we can crash harder with your invidious blows the next.'

And I sat, creature, and I thought these things, and I cradled his head, and then I wailed. I looked at the sky and I wailed a primal scream, a defeated moan coming from somewhere deeper than my gut. I raised my voice, and thought at the time that it was possible, in an attempt to shatter the sun, to blot it out with the fury of my depths. For, I thought my hate and hurt, with the intensity of a thousand purple suns, could heat all humanity. Why would we need the yellow eye to taunt us each day? I looked up at the eye and wailed my primal scream, hoping it would turn into a spear and with its sharp point smash the cruel eye and dash it across the cold universe. But, it was all in vain; the sun still exists. And, when I realized the sun would continue to iridesce and light humanity's way, I sat and continued to scream. And behind the pain and anguish of my new scream, if a scream could project words, it said without equivocation: Life is a bullet with the deadliest of intentions from the moment it is fired. It cauterizes upon entry so as to look harmless, but is so messy upon exit that it demolishes any semblance of what we once were. When the bullet is finished with us, we will not even recognize ourselves. My scream spoke all these words in one high, piercing stab of anguish. I sat screaming at the sun until finally I was carried, dragged away as dead as the man who lay lifeless on the ground.

I spent the next few years beyond the reach of human dimension. There is nothing else to say of that time. Oh, sure, creature, after a period of what doctors deemed 'insanity,' I did try to reemerge, but my convalescence was thwarted. Life was too repulsive, and I remained a shell of what I once was, and only my eyes, serving as anachronisms to my ghostlike body, retained some ancient vibrancy. I wish I could gouge them out. I have no need to see, and my eyes betray me. Their subtle chicanery tricks people into thinking there is life left in me, the same way a shed snakeskin startles the person who comes upon it in the wild because it retains form, much as an oasis forces a barren desert to teem with life—only it's all mirage, scenery for a play never to be written, let alone acted out.

The creature noticed that although there was a numbness swirling at the surface of her eyes, they retained a docile form of life, but the creature could not explain the divergent depths nor the network of emotions. They were unmolded clay, exiled potentates, seeds of a great oak, and they invoked both pity and reverence.

The dim light hurried on, reflecting the woman's past, allowing the creature little time to analyze or fathom exactly what the woman's eyes portended.

Time passed; proceeded to hastily unwind weeks, seasons, and years in a continuous blur, all seeming like a single winter day. Then, something happened. The place where the hurt resides started to harden, and scab. The wound did not heal; it just stopped bleeding. One day I awoke, stretched my arms, yawned, and realized the boulder that had been placed upon my chest was miraculously lifted. I say lifted, but in truth it shifted, or even transformed into something else. At any rate, the reprieve from such bondage felt invigorating, and, during my reprieve, creature, I did meet another man, and, to a degree, this meeting aroused the faculties within me to, if not reawaken, at least rise to the surface of my lifeless body and make me feel like I had rejoined the ranks of the living.

The modicum of vigor I enjoyed was short-lived. It did not take long before I realized the hurt I had suffered in the past had transformed itself, become active, and I sought to recreate the scene or act of love that had caused my body such transitory joy, all in an effort to rid my body of the hurt it now possessed. Is it possible? Can hurt become so powerful it tries to consume itself in an attempt not to exist? Privy to my hurt's intention, I quickly realized I chose this new man because he appealed to an emotion akin to sentimentality or nostalgia. He reminded me of the man who had been ripped away; he reminded me of my dead ideal. I humored him for a time because he had similar qualities and because even going through the motions of something that is a simulacrum or a rehearsal for the real thing is better than staying locked in a room. Eventually, we were married. I entered the contract vowing to the pretext of semblance for a love once lived. I do not know what he saw in me. I was not much of a wife. Ghosts rarely make good wives. At the beginning, I envisioned him as my former lover, which made the situation bearable, but then the emotional strain of pretending became too much, and the constant reminder of how beneath my ideal this man was began to gnaw at me. Nor would it be fair to have had him meet such a pedestaled ideal. It would have cheapened the death of former love. For a time, we went on this way. I was unhappy, but felt like I warranted such unhappiness. He was content for things to continue as they were. Some men require so little.

If hurt can become so painful to bear it tries to expunge itself, the same can be said of artificial life. Pretending to live had become so daunting a task I sought ways to return to my former pain. At least, in my extremities, I was not feigning emotion nor betraying myself and the love I once enjoyed. I wanted to be the sole proprietor of such destitution and loneliness—and by returning to such a hurt, as an empty vessel, I would live out my days true to a love passed on. I would use any excuse or means to get back to such an awful state of being. And, so, it should not shock you, creature, to find me, on a certain day, rummaging through some of my husband's things. What I found, however, rattled me more than I anticipated. While ransacking his room, I stumbled (I say stumbled, but we do not really stumble upon things. Events, like stars, are aligned in their exact orbits long before they take place, and how long this event was kindled, waiting for me to enter its orbitary realm, only the maker of such salient stars could know) upon some pictures in his desk's bottom drawer.

The pictures were of me and my dead love. Unbeknownst to us at the time, they were taken when we were walking hand in hand in this very park. There were numerous pictures. Some captured us laughing, others showed us talking. In some, we were silently staring at each other or ahead, or at some object obscured from view. In each picture, the preeminent factor was the happiness on our faces and the contentment of being in the other's presence. The drawer was full of such images.

Obviously the perpetrator had hidden, otherwise he would not have captured such intimate moments. Simply realizing this pair of voyeuristic eyes was present the entire time made those moments of great joy feel cheap. Then it dawned on me, and the hair on my neck stood erect, and my heart almost burst from my breast as I noticed the angle of the pictures was the same as from which the bullet was fired. The thought arose that perhaps my husband was the very miscreant who had fired the bullet, or, he knew, and was in collusion with, the cold-blooded murderer. Do you know what unbridled anger arises in the damned when they even consider such things? It is the gall spilling from incensed bowels, the bitterest dregs from the bitterest cup drunk, when they think they have found from where the source of their hell and the destroyer of their blissful state of being springs.

I threw down the pictures in such a rage that they scattered up and out of the drawer and one flipped over, and there on the back was a date, etched in black against the white backdrop, and the date shone like a dark mole on a bright face, drawing my eye. I picked up the picture and studied the date and then turned the photo over and looked at myself and my love walking hand in hand. The picture was taken exactly one month from the day my love died. My curiosity intensified to see if there were more dates on the backs of other pictures, or, particularly, to see if the fateful day of death had been photographed. If the picture I held represented one month from the day, and he had a stack, possibly he had the photograph of that day. It is strange how my embittered gall relaxed when a curiosity overtook me to discover how much sicker and dehumanized I could become by continuing to search the pictures.

What did I hope to find? Or, did I already know what I would see? It was like witnessing an accident from a distance. You know, as you approach, the smartest course of action is to look away, but you can't. Morbid curiosity binds your vision to the scene, and no appeal to prudence can draw back the metallic fingers whose clasp forces your eyes to remain wide open. And, then, you are upon the scene and you see the horse with the broken neck and bone protruding through its skin, and you feel queasy, and you wonder why you had to look, but it is too late to try to understand your motives because the recoil from the image of bone protruding through neck has already altered your state of mind, and, so, you cannot come back to the insouciant view of the world, and in a way you are glad you will never make it back to such frivolousness, regardless of how sick you now feel.

And, so, I grabbed the pictures and began throwing them aside to reach the bottom of the stack. I had to see at what date the pictures would end. My fingers could not work fast enough. How many pictures did he take? Finally, I got to the bottom of the stack, and, sure enough, the final pictures taken were of the execrable moment after the bullet entered my love's brain and after his body crashed to the ground and I cradled his head in my lap. How repulsive. How utterly repulsive to see myself through the eyes of the one who had killed my love. And how sickening, distorted, and frail I looked sitting on the ground with the bleeding head of my only true love cradled in my lap, with my solemn stare at an empty sky, and with my eyes frozen in the very act of asking 'why.'

Oh, what a sickening feeling. But the sensation was also strange, not quite the insipient anger I had earlier felt; it was not the engulfing rage that makes one want to lash out against anything; instead, it was a pathetic disgust for the first moment that had caused this newer moment to become a reality. It was disgust that love's moment of death in my life had been captured on camera. That such a moment, unbearable and beyond mortal comprehension, was, after all, cheapened by a few pictures of my total bereavement—a couple of still lifes someone could hang on a wall. Are these still lifes what the gods look at when they divine our fates? Do they see us in such frozen light? Are we no more than subjects for their art? If so, none of us could implore from them an ounce of pity. If they could watch like this photographer (my husband, I am sure) such moments, and not rend the very sky into pieces, but rather with total indifference freeze frame the wounded and hurt and cause them to look so distorted and sickly, who would want anything to do with them? They must get a kick out of our weaknesses, out of our hurts that seem so trivial to them.

With these thoughts coursing through my mind, and with the animus of bitterness surging into my throat, my anger completed its cycle as the acidic quality of its bile began to consume itself, and, within minutes, all my hurt, anguish, and grief turned into the only thing it could: Total apathy. How else does one live with the very destroyer of one's hope and love? My husband: The bullet.

I put the pictures back, but left the drawer disorganized, and walked away feeling more numb than I had when I entered the room. Numbness presents itself in degrees—the totally numb can become even more so. I heard a door creak open as I entered the hallway. I went downstairs to meet my husband. What would he do if he found out I had looked through the drawer, or, did he want me to find those pictures? Why else would he leave them where he knew I would sooner or later come upon them?

I stumbled down the stairs and greeted him with the sardonic smile I had lately made mine. He noticed my rubicund cheeks and mistook my venting anger for excitement to see him—and simpleton that he is—thought the color imbued my pallid face with a touch of classical beauty. We talked about nothing in particular, but what struck me most about the conversation was how easy it was to envision him dying a gruesome death one moment, and, yet, the next, I could answer his questions with utter indifference and a smile. As a byproduct of my new numbness, my anger did not betray me. I could remain a lifeless outer shell and inside still wish upon him a cruel death. I wanted to kill him, it is true. I considered how easy it would be to grab the knife from the kitchen counter when his back was turned and lunge at his vitals, puncturing his chalky flesh with razor-sharp precision. The thought died in transit, alerting me that such a course of action would never come to fruition. And in a twist I thought impossible, my numbness was transforming the anger his face now invoked. Staring into the repugnant mass of flesh and features filled my breast with a happiness I had not felt for years, I was starting to love to hate him. I felt invigorated by the rancor swelling to epic proportions within my breast.

My husband went upstairs to change his clothes, and, as I sat alone in the kitchen, I wondered whether he would notice the disarrayed drawer, if he would find out I had rummaged through the pictures and discovered his horrible secret. I did not care. My complete numbness, coupled with hatred, had become my power. What could he do if he found out I knew he murdered my love? Could he kill a woman who had already died a thousand lonesome deaths? Sure, he could stop my heart from beating, or halt my brain from receiving oxygen, but, for me, capricious life's final leaf had fallen long ago, and the torpid sap of nostalgia from days past had long since dried and hardened.

He came back down after awhile, and he did mention the drawer. As a matter of fact, it was the first thing he asked about upon re-entering the kitchen. He wanted to know what right I thought I had to pilfer through his possessions. They did not belong to me. I did not answer. I did not care to answer. So many things I could have said about violation, and who had what rights, but it seemed so trite and abstract to argue at such a moment and with a man who had destroyed my very world. We sat in the incipient silence. His eyes, the eyes of a cold-hearted killer— dark and intense—deadlocked across the table with mine—the trembling eyes of two dying stars. He then proceeded to murmur: 'You're a wall. Within your body, there is no beating heart.' To which I angrily replied, 'I'm all heart. One giant, throbbing, broken heart.' He laughed and said I have always been and always will be nothing more than a rose wall: Beautiful on the outside, but lifeless underneath all its ostentatiousness.

After a few more moments, he said he was going upstairs, that he was tired, that he'd had a long day of work, that it is not easy to support both of us, that he was going to bed and I could join him if I wished. I watched him leave, and, as he ascended the stairs, could not help but wish him dead. But then I thought death would be too easy and too pleasant of an outcome to wish on him, and instead I wished him life. Yes, the only retribution I could afflict upon him was to wish him alive and miserable. If anyone were to enjoy the coziness of death's warm embrace, it would be me, not him.

He climbed the last stair and disappeared from my view. I sat in the somber room and thought about what next to do. It would be easy for me to get up and leave, just walk out the door and not look back, not even in memory, simply try and erase my crushed heart and hope for the scar that would appear in its place. Besides, how tiring and difficult a task it would prove to climb those stairs and venture near such a repulsive and atavistic being.

I sat and watched as the daylight waned, and listened as the crickets ushered in night. The house began to fill with shadows. I gathered myself, and, in my final heroic attempt at immolation, decided to make my living death complete. I crawled up the stairs on all fours, like a dog, too weak in the soul to stand up. I reached the top stair in a cold sweat, and, for a moment, collapsed from pure exhaustion. Regaining my legs, I stumbled along the never-ending hallway, and, staggering, placed one hand on the room's doorpost. I leaned against the frame, using it as a crutch. I stuck my head and shoulders across the threshold and looked in on him. I cast a searing gaze his way and as it hit its mark, as I glared into his horrible eyes, I wished him life; with the dying embers of my only life, I wished him long, dreadful, painful existence, and I knew right then and there my living death and his long life would be the only revenge and retribution I could exact for the love I had lost—the love he had murdered. And, as he said, 'I thought you might make it up here,' I shut off the light and entered the room the way a cadaver is slid back into the mortuary's dank shelf. The words in my head, the thoughts flooding my brain as I walked deeper into the darkness, the light explained to the creature, *are the simple words of the defeated, not of hate, but the gnawing and numbing moan of sorrow.*

What a coffin the universe must make.
A velvet backdrop draped over cosmic slate.
The planets as pallbearers shoulder the weight.

A solemn procession trudging, in unison, the solar system's
circle to deposit the lifeless giant in the graveyard of light gone
extinct—the brilliant black hole.

As if my entire life and all its agony could be summed up in a quaint verse. When life loses meaning and becomes a debased exercise in sorrow, even poetry fails to explain. But, what am I saying? No one would understand.

The light completed unraveling the crestfallen woman's story. The weary creature sat with solemnity upon the woman's lap—the lap that had cradled the dying head of her ineffable love; the lap that had caught each spurt of his blood. The creature recognized the similarities between the woman's awful predicament and that of the old man, in that sorrow had carved a deep pit, a black hole, within her heart, and, at the bottom of all her digging, she had found nothing but the cold dirt of endless suffering. However, for the woman, unlike the old man, sorrow had rotted away any desire to look for further meaning or knowledge or a return to vibrant life. Sorrow had pushed the woman past her breaking point, beyond her mental capacity, and she naturally snapped and did not wish to be put together again.

The creature knew if it could tell her about the incorrigible old man, about the light, the fire he was bound to reach at the bottom of his pit—it knew if the man had found the end of such a hole—that kind of knowledge could lift up the woman's hanging hands and support her feeble knees; it could help her abandon her reckless path and pick up the shovel of affliction once more to keep digging. *But, oh, what a fatal mistake it had made,* the creature thought to itself. It had left the man's side too soon. Sure, when beside the man it did not need to witness the outcome of his digging to know the man would meet his desired end and strike fire or tunnel through and find light, but now that it had left his side and ventured into the world, the creature's confidence had weakened. As if the deeper the creature delved into this new world, and the farther the distance from the old man spanned, the more the creature's conviction and purpose became impaired, and it began to wonder if it was worth the effort for the woman to continue her quest for meaning. Perhaps she was right in succumbing to the afflicting numbness of life. There is, after all, a certain serenity in falling apart.

Its shattered confidence, however, would not deter the creature from trying to bring the woman auspice. And, as it thought about the old man and his digging, a resilient seed of hope sprang within its tiny breast, and a confidence in the old man, and in its own quest, returned. It wanted to tell the woman she could hold fast and keep seeking meaning in her life, and it would return. It wanted to let her know that perhaps her suffering would end, or serve a purpose beyond the callow comprehension of this life, but the woman would not listen, and, if she had, it would not have mattered, because the entirety of the creature's thoughts amounted to nothing more than the incessant buzzing ejaculating from its tiny mouth.

The woman, her eyes as brittle as the aspen's fallen leaves, looked down on the small creature, and she picked it up. She cusped it in her right hand with assurance and whispered upon her fingernails and into the crevices of her fingers, "Fly away, little creature; fly away while you still can. Flee the city." Once said, the woman lifted her hand toward the breeze and gently released the creature into the careening stream of wind.

The creature glided up and away from the woman, and, as it did, looked at her slightly upraised alabaster hands and her sad eyes and her flowing red hair, and it thought how no image had ever looked so queenly, so beautiful, or stood so much like a sentinel for the ages as this woman: Her pleading attitude spoke of so much pain and suffering; her supine hands, like a marble goddess, begging for life's mercy; her eyes, the sad reminder of too much useless pain; and her hair, covered in the red drops of heaven's spilt blood, gently dripping in the autumn breeze.

The woman had seen much, had suffered much, and, as the creature looked down upon her, it felt racked by a pang that started in its heart and spread through its entire being. It wanted to return to the woman, but did not wish to further intrude upon such sad and austere beauty; besides, it did not know if it could take the further unraveling of such light. Just then, the breeze picked up and shuttled the creature away at a rapid pace. But, before it left the scene of the accident, the place where this woman's love had died, it looked one last time at the sad lady who sat guarding a king's tomb with her questioning hands and eyes raised toward an empty sky.

All Over a Bowl of Bitter Beans

OVER the next few weeks, the creature did not fare much better. Between the furious onslaught of wing-drenching rain—forcing it to cling to the undercarriage of whatever leaf, rock, or shrub it could find to avoid the brunt of the storm's precipitation—and the large nets random people used to chase after it, these were weeks the creature wished to forget. Naturally, as it unknowingly passed through life's common vicissitudes, it wondered why it had ever left the old man's side. Up to this point, the only memorable occasions away from the man had been of extreme discomfort or filled the creature's soul with banal sorrow and doubt.

Whilst wandering, the creature divided its life into three distinct periods. First: The time of its juvenescence spent in the presence of the magnanimous old man. Of that time, the creature reminisced about the wonderful knowledge of the man, and the long and tedious days of hard but rewarding toil (of course, the creature was more a spectator), and the never-ending stories the man related about his strange and squalid youth. All these things the creature thought about now—imbued with time's uncanny ability to glorify the past—with the sturdiest recollection and most palpable of joys, and it longed for more such experiences. It was these recollections, thought the creature, that reminded it why it felt the urge to tell the world the old man's story in the first place, and these recollections spurred it on in the face of opposition.

The second distinct period (or stage of growth): The creature's brush with the harsh realities of an unremitting world. The creature still shuddered when it thought about the horrible time spent in the presence of the irascible, unkempt man who shuttled it across the river. The creature felt the wrenching ache in its abdomen when it thought, even momentarily, about the tragic time in the presence of the austere but abeyant beauty of the woman whose pain seemed as ancient as time itself. Whereas time usually heals mortal wounds, it had yet to place its bandage upon the open gash this stage of life caused the creature. However painful, the creature identified two important truths from this period.

The first verity perceived was how sorrow and pain acted upon the vastness of life's matter and compressed it into a heavy and distinct mass of tightly wound molecules. The creature had no analogy or metaphor apropos for this compression, but its thoughts reverted to an image of a large river funneling through a small gorge, and how the rushing water builds pressure and speed at the point of ingress, then how the water slows again and spreads to flow shallow and tranquil at the point of egress—sorrow and pain forced life's flow to function in a similar manner: Intense and deep. The second verity the creature recognized was how sorrow and pain were not one-time occupants of their host, but prodigals whose inevitable return was not celebrated with the killing of the fatted calf. *One could beat sorrow into remission,* the creature thought, *but its depressing affects never fully defected and trigger moments caused it to swell again within the host with ferociousness similar to, but not as powerful as, its initial blow.* Of a certainty, the creature could identify these truths about sorrow and pain; it frankly felt uncertain as to what it should do with this knowledge.

The third period, the current interval, was a time of lackadaisical, directionless wandering with no real destination. If creatures were afforded such experiences as mid-life crises, this period would qualify. Of late, the creature felt harried by its desire to return to the simple life. Always, this desire to return to the old man was combated and suppressed by the conflicting desire and longing to impart the stories of the venerable old man on the inhabitants of whatever region the creature advanced upon. Persistent but flickering desire filled the creature's breast with the hope that maybe someone would listen, maybe someone would benefit, and maybe someone would understand when it opened its treasure-trove of past experiences.

Alas, these hopes were in vain and came to naught. Most people viewed the creature as a pest, a nuisance, and its attempts of promulgation were met with vehement swats of the hand. Nearly all misunderstood what it sought when it entered a room and attempted to dissect the light emitted by the bulbs. Almost all viewed the creature as a destructive being, an outcast spawn of the devil still aching from its august expulsion and incessantly waging war on this world's light.

Of course, such thinking is erroneous, but, for his part, how would a human comprehend the moth's annoying but gentle brush and patter with the skein of un-spooling light escaping from the being, or that the bulb is an attempt to fathom the history of the occupants themselves and of the place, respectively. Oh, the poor, misunderstood creature; so desperate to at least find one soul with which it could share all the goodness stored in its abdomen.

At this pivotal time of want, the creature abandoned the stalk of the common mullein on which it had remained fastened for an hour, and flew into the open window of a house belonging to a middle-aged man it had seen the day before walking down the street. A man, who, consequently, during his weekly walk not only didn't mind the creature's fluttering wings near his face, but also did not threaten to roll and use as a weapon the paper he held—an incontrollable and justifiable reaction of almost all human beings.

Entering the man's house through a window, the creature first noticed the barren white walls and the messy kitchen. There were dishes piled in the two sinks. The floor was covered in a film of dust, and tiny balls of hair, lint, and cobwebs infested each of the corners. Closer inspection of the barren walls revealed small black scars of nail holes that had once hung pictures or decorations. The cabinet doors were swung open and manifested the meager sustenance of the middle-aged man, as there was a loaf of bread in a plastic bag, some canned foods scattered on the shelf, and nothing more. The sparse cabinets appeared as if someone had ransacked in haste, and, seizing only the necessities, left what remained for the rodents and rust. In the center of the kitchen sat the room's lone furnishings: An old, dirty oak table with one wobbly leg, and an accompanying chair—with its corresponding wobble. The empty chair and table resembled a captive's hard exterior gloss beneath the interrogating glow of the low-hanging overhead light.

In the kitchen's corner, the middle-aged man attended to his boiling soup, stirring when necessary, and once in a while checking the palatableness of the concoction. The creature watched the man grab one of the dirty bowls from the sink, rinse it with water, and then dry it using his shirt. The man repeated the process with a spoon, and then poured what looked like some kind of bean soup, minus the vegetables, into the bowl and placed it, along with the spoon, on the table. The discarded pot joined the others in the dirty dish pile. The man reached into the open cabinet and tore a piece of bread from the loaf, before sliding it back to its previous spot. He placed the piece of stale bread on the table, sat down in the wobbly chair, and lurched forward to be closer to the soup. The man dipped his spoon and culled a steaming spoonful. After swallowing his first bite, the man spotted the creature hovering in a crook of the kitchen. Without sarcasm or pretentiousness, he invited the creature to join him for dinner. Then, chortling a bit, the man said, "I would invite you to pull up a chair, but, as you can see, I don't have any other than this rickety one. It isn't everyday a visitor happens to drop by unannounced." The man slouched over and blew on his next spoonful. The creature, with an abdomen full of presentiment, remained in its sheltered nook.

By now, the creature had all but abandoned any attempt of speaking with humans. From frustrated experience, it understood the pointlessness. What an awful feeling to grapple with a gnawing truth and not have any means of expression. The creature now thought it better to suffer the initial disappointment of remaining silent rather than the dejected failure of attempting to speak. The man continued to blow on the spoonful of soup as vapors of steam rose in spiraled wisps and disappeared into the light. Then, once again, displaying behavior contrary to the customary nature of the majority of humans with which the creature had so far become acquainted, the man lifted a steaming bean from his spoon and placed it at the far edge of the table .

"I do not wish to offend even the least of God's creatures," said the man in a tone of condemnation, yet full of sincerity. "Who knows, but some angel may be recording this episode in the book of life, and, perhaps this moment, even this miniscule moment between you and I, creature, matters."

The creature would not be inveigled into another trap and fall for the subterfuge and sophistries of human deceit. Its evolved survival mode had imprinted it with two valuable assets when confronting humans. First, let the light reveal what it may, and, second, look for harmless traits and characteristics. Once discerned, the creature could determine its proper course of action. And, in the case of the middle-aged man, the light's qualities implied his harmlessness, and the creature gathered from his behavior that although the man might not necessarily be docile, he feared acting in a malicious manner. The creature fluttered toward the table, and nearing the low-hanging light, cast its behemoth shadow on the blank walls. It landed upon the offered bean, and, in an attempt to befriend the man, pretended to nibble.

The man felt happy to have company. It had been so long since anyone had come to visit. He placed another bean near the creature and encouraged it to eat as he did the same. Elated by the friendly demeanor of the man, the creature instinctually, and against its own credo, tried to speak, and although its effort was met with failure, it noticed that the emitted grinding noise did not sound as harsh or foul as usual, and a discernable syllable or two snuck out. The man heard the droning, and almost thought the creature was trying to speak.

"Creature, if I did not know better, I would say you are trying to communicate with me." The creature grew animated. It thought to itself, *finally a chance to unload everything locked within*, and it tried again to speak, but to no avail. The horrible noise had returned with vigor, and the man, who had sat piqued on the edge of his chair straining to hear audible words, slouched back deflated by the awful sound. "I knew I was imagining things. I need to get out more."

The man reverted to blowing on his soup. He was disappointed the creature could not speak. He became so distraught he altogether forgot about his soup and the task of eating. The spoon, limp, dropped back into the bowl, and the man slipped into a mood of profound reverie. As he slipped further away, his effluvium of ebullient light began to meander toward the starving creature. The light possessed a strange quality. It arrived in spurts of intensity, and then mellowed out. Almost as if the light worried about overloading the creature, or as if the moments were too intense to be transmitted in any way other than quick and ardent flashes, followed by slow cyclical build-ups, working their way up to the intensity of the quick flashes.

The creature had never come in contact with such a strange, random, ambiguous type of light. But, new experience neither discouraged nor vexed the creature beyond its comprehension. It had practiced deciphering the light people shed forth, and it had started to hone its craft of unraveling the messages coded in sporadic moments and memories, and it had managed a method of piecing together the fragmented shards of life into a single working pattern. And what did the random light rolling forth from the man bent over his soup and lost in reverie say? It told of three recurring dreams: Two he had while sleeping, and one he kept having while awake. Asleep or awake, there was no escaping the awful reality, or non-reality, of the dreams.

II

The man stared into his bowl, and, listening to the light's continuous hum, recalled a time when he was young and naïve. Back then, his mother used to prepare his soup. It was a special treat for a little boy to come home from school on a cold winter's day and find the steaming soup waiting. He would shed his layers of clothing as he entered the house and run into the kitchen with the smell of basil or tomato permeating his nostrils. The bowl would be waiting for him on the table. On special occasions, his mother would prepare his favorite—alphabet soup. How, as a child, he loved to look at those letters floating in the tomato paste. He would grow animated and fill his spoon in an attempt to capture as many letters or possible words into his mouth, and then he would look at them as they swayed on the spoon and see what he could spell, and without ever worrying about burning his tongue, would laugh and swallow them whole.

Of course, for the boy, the enchantment of these moments came in part because he knew his mother was not supposed "to waste"—as his father used to remind her when he came home early—their meager savings on spoiling the child. The boy knew his mother would be punished if his father found out, and he knew, with an overflowing heart of kindness, his mother feared the disappointment of her child much more than the lashing out of her husband. The boy knew, too, that as she watched him perform his ritualistic consumption of the soup, her eyes would light up. They tried to keep the ritual their secret. What it cost her, what pains she bore to assure him some blissful moments in an otherwise blighted youth, the child was too young to fully grasp, but the token of her sacrifice the boy carried with him into adulthood.

The slow, revolving light explained all this to the creature as the man stared into his soup. Then, an ardent flash of light darted at the creature, and, with pulsing intensity, shocked the creature with its power. "It's a lie," declared the light. As quickly as the pulse revealed the man's thought, it was gone. The creature regained its composure and then watched and prepared itself as the earlier, more torpid light continued its snail-like crawl away from the man.

When the torpid light reached the creature once again, it explained the meaning behind the flash. It explained how the man could not remember correctly the childhood memory of his mother. How, to the man's discontent, and, try as he might, the memory had become embellished and apocryphal. How, each time the man tried to extract from his childhood moments of bliss, his memory rejected the request and continued to recollect false moments. All the man had hoped for were succinct visions of his fondest memories, but his psyche continued to deny him the pleasure. The light continued to explain to the creature that although the boy did receive, parsimoniously, an extra meal or two from his mother, they was nothing like the elaborate illusions now remembered. His poor father never castigated him or his mother over such modest luxuries. While the man sat staring into his soup, wearing a blank expression and brooding over his lost memories, the light continued to fall in rhythm upon the creature, disclosing further the falsified memory:

The boy scarfed his spoonfuls with ardor. Each time he pulled the spoon from the soup, brimming with letters, he watched with wanton eyes as the excess tomato paste dripped back into the bowl, taking with it a letter or two. The boy pictured the bowl of soup as a brooding cauldron, and he the omniscient soothsayer preparing to cast a spell or create a charm, each letter or combination of conjured letters the necessary elixir. He imagined the possibilities of words he could string together with each spoonful from such a full cauldron, and, as the spoon neared his hungry mouth, he would recite the letters in the random order in which they appeared and envision them as some strange language only witches or warlocks could understand. The mother would stand near her boy, and laugh or smile.

Then, as the lethargic light uncoiled the man's strange repast, another random dart of furious light unfurled itself upon the creature, the velocity and force of the blow causing it to cringe. This time, the flash of light did not just say, "It's a lie" and then abscond, for no sooner had the light hit the creature than the creature found itself observing the most strange and barren land, and more: It actually found itself amid the ruinous landscape, as if transported by the light.

Now, it needs be interjected, light utilized numerous mediums with which to reveal truths to the creature, none of which were necessarily words. The creature had often thought about how futile and what a poor medium words represented in projecting the ruminations of the mind, and how short the metaphor falls in untangling even the most inherent of thoughts. This new vision demonstrated to the creature the impotence of metaphors, words, and even images when attempting to portray or capture such overwhelming feelings. The creature remained amazed by the differing powers of the piercing emotion and the clarity thrust upon it by the current vision. The light achieved more than paint the most vivid picture of the man's dream: It recreated the recollection, placing the creature within the man's memories. The creature did not simply view scenery, then; it saw scenery as witnessed by the man, and felt emotion as experienced by him. And, suddenly, while the creature surveyed the bleak surroundings, the light divulged the man's dream.

III

I am walking amid the rubble of destroyed buildings that once made up the city. Everything is coated in a still-ashen gray, and, more than just a shade, the gray represents something elemental: It symbolizes something primitive. I know it; I can feel the visceral, almost biological power of this gray that has always been present, but only with its tumefaction has become a concern. What it is I can't wrap my mind around, can't quite express in words, but it feels somewhat like a perishing dream, and to study the gray induces the same feeling I experience upon awaking from a blissful sleep, a sleep brimming with euphoric emotion and exalted scenery, and I want to remember it, want to recapture it; I want to know what caused me to stir with such passion, such emotion, but all I experience is the emptiness of forevermore departing sleep. And, I know where I am now: This waking place would not be so horrible if it were not for the contrast of the place I just left. The feeling harbored deep within the gut upon waking from such a slumber; the feeling of what could be, what is possible, and then the stifling reality of what actually is: This is the feeling associated with the gray. I acutely sense all the stunted possibilities and crippled ambitions that lie beneath its ashen coat.

I stumble on. I know I have been here before, but when, and under what circumstances, remain mysteries. I don't dare look to the left or the right. Strewn across the street are bodies; bodies that won't stop wheezing, struggling for breath, writhing, coughing up the gray; bodies that are wandering, lost, or hidden beneath an inch of thick dust; bodies that are yanking at their own skin, vomiting up their own entrails, stretching out their emaciated hands in pleas of help—all of them beyond help.

Dust is falling from the sky, making it difficult to breathe. It stings the lungs. It burns the eyes. I am holding onto a railing; it is my only safety against losing my way. Where the sun should be, there is a foul alabaster ring that casts a futile light which hardly penetrates the gray. Ashes like identical snowflakes keep falling. I don't know what kind of cosmic disturbance has caused this condition, but, as I look down at my hands, I realize even my flesh has turned a bitter gray, and I know my innards, my heart, and my vitals have also mutated into the same dank grayness.

It is terminal.

I keep walking, my destination set by a firm grasp on the railing. I come to a dilapidated building whose outer wall is not yet reduced to rubble. I can't see inside the doorway. It is darker than a cave. I am expecting two primitive glowing yellow eyes to look back at me, but they don't. I want to walk on, but am drawn to this place, and the railing, which is my only sure navigational guide, leads inside. There is something I must see; I must come to know. I do not like the tingle rising in my gut. Instinct tells me to run, to let go of the railing and take my chances in the charcoaled day, but I am riveted to the spot. My second instinct takes over, the thanatotic instinct that does not fear fear, the one that revels in it, that knows by facing fear it has faced the worst of fear's creations: Uncertainty in man. It guides me as I enter the blacker-than-pitch doorway.

In the offing, there is a voice: Sonorous, cutting, full of emotion. Like the ocean's waves, it comes constant and crashing, crashing, crashing in canorous rhythm. I continue to walk along a dark hallway. I don't know whether the building still exists. Once I walked into it, everything peripheral turned dark and unreal, and I sensed the voice and the shallow light ahead like a tunnel: The voice is the light I am moving toward. I continue walking, only my feet have trouble finding where to step; I use the railing to reassure myself of direction and balance.

The voice grows louder, boisterous, full of emotion. The echo is overpowering in this quiet, dreamlike place. It sounds the way the trumpet must when it startles the dead from their silent graves. The dark cavern widens, and I am looking into a large room, capacious and cold. Candles adorn prickets and are burning a white-gray stain on each behemoth pillar. Gothic buttresses protrude from the tops and bottoms of the pillars, and fine damasks hang from metal rods in the aisles. Row upon row of hand-chiseled and elaborate wooden pews is filled with people. They have come to hear the voice. I know this. Some are rocking back and forth. Some are in the attitude of genuflecting, chanting, or moaning. I cannot hear the people, and where their faces should be are dark, gray features. I turn away. I look past the pillars, beyond the multitudinous rows of people, and spot, beneath the gray and translucent stained-glass window fused into the metallic story of creation and the flood and the exodus, directly underneath the glass visage of a man with a long white beard and outstretched arms holding a wooden staff, rebuking the receding waters of the sea; there, directly underneath this image, clutching the pulpit, is the genesis of the voice: It is a man adorned in sacerdotal robes.

The man is animated. He does not belong here. Nothing here is animated. Everything takes place in muffled silence and with drawn-out movements, but this man does not seem to be influenced by the place. He turns his head from one end of the room to the other, his body vacillating. He is making sure his voice reaches everyone. He is entranced by the power of his own speech. Every once in a while, he loosens his grip from the outer edge of the wooden rostrum and slams his fist down upon the pulpit. I cannot see his face very well, so I continue to draw nearer until the railing ends. I no longer require it. I can see what it has guided me to. I let go. I come within ten paces of the pulpit, and stop.

The robed man is facing the other way. I watch as his body rocks back and forth, as his turning head, with the consistency of a sprinkler, makes its way toward me. I see the corner of an eye, the black lashes, then, he completes his turn and I am looking directly at him. A peculiar thing happens as I look at his face. I do not know how to explain it, and perhaps it is beyond the means of description, but as I stare at him I nearly disintegrate, dissolve, abscond the very matter of body and melt into atoms of nothingness if such a thing is possible, and all because of his eyes.

His eyes are not gray like everything else in this place. His eyes are the most peaceful and live green, the color of two shining emeralds, and, within each, at the center of the pupil, is the most vivid and piercing red, the color of jasper, and the red attaches itself to the center of his green eyes and then in tiny vein-like shafts spreads out to the edges like two red octopi clinging to two large green stones, large arms spreading out and tentacles expanding around the green stones in an attempt to devour them whole. So were his eyes, and when they looked at you, you could not help but feel like the helpless green stone swallowed whole.

Oh, how this priest flaunted those eyes, the way he abused such power. With them, he laughed me to scorn, seared my soul; and when he perceived their effect, he paused, and let his gaze rest upon me more fully. Then, he stopped preaching. He slowed his undulating body so everything seemed in slow motion. The worshippers did not move, did not make a sound, and his silent gaze spoke its searing jest at me for a moment, then began another turn.

When his gaze moved away, the room grew noisy and filled with the muddled and shuffling sounds of knees scraping, hands and foreheads hitting the wooden benches, and the man's voice regaining its sonorous tones. The echo came back to the spacious building, and things continued as if nothing had happened. But, something had happened between me and the priest. A transaction of sorts had taken place, and I was his now, a victim of his power. With one glance he had surveyed my whole life, weighed and balanced it, and I knew he had found me wanting. In those eyes, there was encapsulated some strange judgment.

I shuffle forward without noticing it. When his eyes make their turn back my way, I am standing directly in front of them. The scarlet center looms larger, until it is omnipresent. The priest continues to preach, and I listen attentively to each word, afraid to fall victim to any warranted, angry gaze. Typical of sermons that prey upon fear following calamity, the priest's words are apocalyptic and carry the weight of destruction, but the words cannot match the intensity of a single look from the scarlet center of his pupils.

In his sermon, the sixth seal has been torn open and catastrophes have been loosed both below man, as the earth's bowels opened up and swallowed the wicked whole, and above man, as the stars refused their light and came crashing down from the heavens. I had heard sermons on the topic before, but they were lavished with such luxuries or provoked by proximate needs to such a degree that the present stood as a barrier to my comprehension of such strange and eccentric future happenings. Even now, as the apocalyptic destruction rages, I cannot fear the angry weather or some ethereal calamity. My gaze is fixed on those oracle eyes; eyes revealing the crux of life's very essence, and it behooves me to know what mystery hides within them. Let the earth have her calamities.

He rolls his head back and to the side for a moment, exposing to the congregation the nape of his neck. He pauses, looks up at the massive picture of the prophet brandishing his menacing staff. Then, he drops his head so that his eyes rest once more upon the congregation. The audience stirs, and I know they, too, are mesmerized by his eyes. The priest has regained vigor and his next words come crashing against every ear. He says he will reveal a secret, but will only unlock a portion because he knows mystery itself must remain enigmatic or else it will annul the healthy anxiety and necessary tension that accompanies not knowing. He says something about how each being is born with equal embryonic or rudimentary capacities to become a god or a devil. He relates how both deities, to a degree, reside within us, and although neither dictates behavior, the divine occupant's influence is easily identified through emotional stirrings and the poignant promptings guiding our lives. He speaks of the double nature of man. He tells us the power and decision lies within us to become a devil or a god, according to which voice we heed. He says there is no such thing as neutral ground and that each inch of cosmic realty, our minds, especially, is either claimed or counterclaimed by the powerful force of good or evil. The sermon leaves no room for objections, not because what is said upholds the truth, but because the words are superfluous in comparison with the axiom located in the eyes fixed upon us, and none of us, regardless of how strong the objection to what is said, would dare object to anything while his gaze rests upon us.

His sermon moves in lacunal lapses to the purification of the earth by fire. He calls the firestorm a time of righteous claiming, a type of territorial cleansing. He does not delve into explanation, does not offer lengthy or even logical arguments as to why things will be, or even how; things simply are or will be, as he says. He issues the congregation a challenge: "If there are any of the wicked, any evildoers, any lovers of darkness among us, let them now step forward."

None identify themselves. And when the aisles remain empty and not a single soul budges, he yells at the top of his lungs, the echo reverberating from all angles, "What do you think, cowards? On the day He does return to burn the earth, to baptize it with fire, who do you think will stand in judgment upon your poor soul, and who could withstand such a baptism?"

His right hand releases its grip on the pulpit and comes hammering down like a gavel's bang upon wood—judgment meted.

"Your soul will burn with the wrath of your own indignation. If you have heeded that devil within, then the searing, seething pain of realizing how wrong you were, and the recognition of how close you were to God—for he never is more than a correct thought away—will scald your mind with the intensity of a thousand glowing suns, and you will wish to annihilate your own soul from existence, but will not be able to do so."

For a moment, he does not say anything. He allows the silence to pervade, and silence at a moment like this causes one to feel guilt. Silence at a moment like this causes guilt to sink deep into the pit of a stomach and wreak havoc on a system.

When the silence has actualized its effect on the congregation, he continues. "And those who heeded that Heavenly Being's knock at the inner door will burn as well. Only, they will not burn with the purging and purifying fire of the wicked. They will burn in the way of a bosom when it is overflowing with love and joy. They will then see Him for what He is because they will be like Him—a consuming and everlasting fire of righteousness."

He does not elaborate. He does not explicate. He simply asks a final question: "And why is this fire the cause of indefatigable torment for one mind and everlasting bliss for another?" Here, the sermon ends. No more is divulged.

Or, perhaps the sermon did continue and I was unable to assimilate the continuation due to bewilderment. I have seen a mother receive news of her child's death and I witnessed how the remainder of the account did not register because the initial piece of information so inundated her with sorrow that only days later she had to ask relatives for details of her son's death. All I know for certain, when the priest is talking about burning, is that his eyes are upon mine. And the only fire I fear is the penetrating gaze when they peer into my soul. This burning sensation that causes me to tremble and convulse is neither the burning of damnation, nor salvation; it is simply the heat from the flame. The burning starts as I watch his pupils contract to pinpoints and the emerald green circumference bleeds into the center of his eye. Then the scarlet rings, in an action that looks almost like a counterattack, expand again and encroach upon the area where the green just filled, and, with each encroachment, the intensity of the burn I am experiencing increases. I am watching with bewilderment and fear when all of a sudden it happens— and, from this point, I can relate what occurs, but what is real and what is imagined is not clear in my own mind:

When the scarlet pupil completes its usurpation of the green iris, I am so near the eye, (right or left, I know not which) that my existence solely comprises me and the penetrating gaze. The voice, and I now realize it is coming from his eyes, speaks softly: "And how about you?" its taunting whisper asks.

"Will the day when the fires of wrath come be 'terrible' or 'great' for you?"

The voice does not remit, but continues the provocations. "I know your fear," it says in a sinister and hushed tone. "You fear you heed the wrong voice."

I find myself walking, drawn toward the eye's center. I see the striation of black amidst the scarlet. The eye continues in susurrations: "You feel the only way to be sure of no offense is by not acting at all."

I am so close I can see my reflection. It is me, I am sure, but there is an aspect of foreignness, a distortion of the image. I can see my mouth move, but it is not of my own volition. I hear myself say the words, "If you will not act, then be acted upon."

No sooner do these words leave my mouth than the scarlet center opens up, and, like a gaping maw, swallows me whole. I pass out.

When I come to, I am suspended in a darkened field. I do not know how long I have been surrounded by this black. Time does not exist. Intensity is the new measure of calculating moments. In the distance, I see a tree on a hilltop. I do not know whether it has always been there, or if it just appeared. Against the bleak background, it boasts a canopy of incandescent green leaves blanketing the branches. The trunk is patched with a corrugated and scaly umber bark that runs down into the dirt. At the heart of the tree is a solitary red apple. I know the apple is precious, and, as I am brought nearer, my desirability for the fruit increases tenfold, until my want, the expediency of possessing the apple, becomes an obsession.

With reckless abandon, I reach out and pluck the apple. As I hold it in my hands, I cannot contain the urge to bite into its flesh. I lift the apple to my mouth and sink my teeth into skin and pulp. Immediately, I am filled with vividness, a feeling of pure being that so excites and overloads me I become unaware of my physical self and give way to a sensation beyond corporeal comprehension, a feeling of total bliss, an interconnectedness with the universe and the power that upholds and animates life. It is a feeling I have never experienced. How long it lasts, I know not, but what intensity!

The sensation begins to wear off, and, as the euphoria abates, I become aware that what I have just done by biting into the apple is irreversible. And, as I slowly masticate the bitten-off piece, I look at the apple and notice that the inside is green and unripe. I suffer a queasy feeling in my gut. Something is amiss. I feel the apple rotting and withering in my hands. Then, the seeds start moving within the desiccated fruit and transform into slithering maggots. I throw the fruit down and spit the remains from my mouth. *What have I done?* I think to myself. I clutch my throat and attempt to induce vomiting. It is too late. I can feel maggots crawling within my body. I can feel them in my bloodstream. I can feel their mucus tickling my throat as they slither down in tracks. I can hear them in my head.

They slide out of my ears and mouth and all my other orifices, leaving a trail of mucous. I feel them at the backs of my eye sockets trying to force an opening into where my eyeballs reside. They leave the bloodstream and start crawling underneath my skin. I can see the bulge of skin move when they move. I am overwhelmed by an incontrollable itch, but, each time I scratch, the action tears the skin and maggots burst out. I can feel them burrowing into my innards. I fall to the ground and am overcome as the maggots begin to funnel from my entire body. I am covered in mucus. I can hear the devouring of what is left of my organs. This army annihilates my skin and starts for my brain. I can hear their chattering teeth as they methodically consume the final remains of my thought processor. I am about to lose consciousness forever when the cacophony of chattering teeth-gnawing relents. I say the teeth stop, but am not correct. The chattering noise simply shifts and becomes a symphony of high-pitched chatter uttering, in unison, one phrase: "I spew thee out."

And, like that, I am spewed from this black place and land on the floor of the beautifully adorned and spacious building—a building I never left. I realize I am a pile of bones, yet, somehow, possess my senses. My heart beats against my rib cage, which sits in a puddle of fluid. The liquid may be blood; I cannot tell because everything except the priest's horrible red eyes is gray. I try to move, but cannot. I am abandoned on the floor. I am aware that a host of faceless people have gathered around me, and, instead of helping me up, are mocking me, pointing their fingers of ridicule and laughing loudly in my face. The bone-clanking noise from their laughter fills the capacious building with a sound like the drumming of locust wings. I lie on the floor, unable to move. The people are still pointing and laughing, but their scorn is emasculated: The bite of a dog whose chain, when pulled taut, keeps it one foot from range of being able to sink its teeth into you. No, there is but one thing that could scorn me here.

The preacher has left the pulpit, veered to his right, walked down the stairs, and now crouches before me, bringing to bear his large scarlet eyes within inches of my beating heart. Oh, the indefatigable heat effectuated by such eyes and gaze! My heart is on the verge of exploding. I feel my bones' marrow boiling. I watch the preacher extend his hand toward my heart. I feel the organ give way, feel the rapid increase of its beat. I am about to disintegrate. It is all I want, to burst into an effervescent cloud of thoughtlessness, to eradicate the pain and anguish and the burning of those searing eyes. Burst open, I scream as the eyes burn into me. Burst, and then, wake up.

A sticky sweat covers my body. My breathing is fast and belabored. It takes minutes to calm down and locate a suitable rhythm. I find it, and, for once, am happier to be awake than back in my dream. Only, I fear this reprieve is transitory and that when night falls, yes, when sleep again overtakes me, I will relive this horrific experience, will have to face once more the scarlet gaze.

IV

The light disappeared. The creature returned from the desolate place and found itself exhausted, but still perched upon the same table and bean. The man still stared at his soup. The creature ascertained that the man's mind was wandering down the labyrinthine roads of former times. Every once in a while, the man would shift in his chair and a wry smile would make its way across his otherwise dour countenance. As the jolted creature recovered from the intensity emitted by the visionary light, as it recovered from close contact with those red eyes that haunted the man's dreams, it noticed the earlier and more customary slow light twirling like a crooked halo around the man's head. This light made its way toward the creature. The man shifted his gaze from the soup, put a hand upon his forehead, and rubbed. The slow light reached the creature and began dispensing its essence in a more mannerly fashion than bursting on the creature and overwhelming it en masse like the jolts of light.

The slow light continued revealing the embellished moment from the man's childhood. The alphabet soup sits again in front of him. His mother watches his spoon dredge up the letters. She stands with a caring posture as her boy looks at the letters, as he imagines the possible words, as he recites the strange cantation, and then devours the spoonful greedily. But, this can only go on for so long, and the soup is about half full and the boy's pace slows. The letters swim with more space in the tomato paste, and the boy is running out of letters and words to devour. Soon, the empty bowl will need washing, and his mother will leave his side. The boy tries to forestall the moment. The torpid light revealed this to the creature when once again a clairvoyant flash of light came streaking, the quick light jolting the small creature; once again, the creature was not simply watching another of the man's visions, but, experiencing it as if it were the man.

V

At the side of a painted-white house lies a closed cellar door. The latch is unhooked and sways upon a rusted hinge that squeaks in the wind. The lock, key intact, lies on the ground. I forget why I am here. I vaguely remember someone has summoned me to retrieve something, but paramount is the overwhelming thought that the summoning was wrought by something residing within the unknown confines of my own mind. I throw open the door and stare into the cloak of blackness. My eyes adjust to the darkness, make out a stairway, and I descend into the maw, the very depths of the lightlessness. I cannot understand why, but with every step into the darkness, I find myself imagining primordial and archetypal images of hell: The smell of brimstone, sulfuric stench, vaporous exhalations of intermittent fumes, the loud crackling and hissing lurch of the odious melodies of damnation, along with the drum of wailing madness from the tortured souls inhibiting such dark places: The indefatigable heat, the hissing motion of the gory fire gliding past, imagining him there, knees buckling, his bestial horns filling the immensity, bloodied skin, burning eyes, carnivorous teeth, ubiquitous abominable laugh, and three-pronged pitchfork as master of all hopelessness. A long pause, and I step further. There is no end to my despair: No end because spiraling infinite, the bottom cannot be reached: It is always racked with insufferable and unending pain, with immolation ever-looming. The mountains will not fall. This cardinal torture, always this unflagging reminder of failure, of loss, of the innocent sufferer: Reliving regret over and again: Thinking these steps might never end. Then, in the moment of extreme necessity, my mind recalls the sagacious words of the old poet, and, like a beacon, my final steps are illuminated:

When any of our faculties retain
A strong impression of delight or pain,
The soul will wholly concentrate on that,
Neglecting any other power it has...

With the recollection, and coinciding moment when I pull the metal chain, the light bulb flips on. My descent into the dank cellar is supplanted by a sparkling room. Just like that, abracadabra, let there be light, and my Gethsemane is dotted with brilliant white-and-yellow flowers speckled across a blithely pink wall. My purgatory is filled with the fake-fruit smell of waxen peaches emanating from a small candle flickering in the corner. And my damnation feels refreshing and crisp, as the summer breeze snakes through the ruffled blinds, caroms off the walls, and ruffles the scattered papers, whispering soft on my skin. The pinnacle of my hell is defined by the most noble and courageous young woman. A woman whose dark hair is splayed, unfurled, where she lies upon the brown- and pink-striped bedspread.

There is no explanation for how I came to this moment. I know as little about this woman and this place as the common spectator, but I do know, through the inundating empathy I feel toward her, that she means something to me, and I know I, too, signify a symbol of import to her. It is as if the animus and anima were playing out a drama in actual forms, as if the soul had surged up and created the image, and now the physical bodies must become helpless observers trapped deep within the anatomy.

I am sitting on the edge of her bed. She is curled up, fetus-like. Her hair is strewn around her like a moat. Tears stream from her eyes and run in rivulets onto her bed, making one last mark before they evaporate. Her back no longer undulates with the weight of whatever made her cry. She grows calm and quiet, serene. Then, without warning, she starts, again, to cry.

I am standing over her. I kneel at her side and look into her eyes. An emotion, like sadness, but more complete, bursts from me. I must try to explain this emotion, but how? It is not common. It is an emotion verging upon blasphemy, an emotion not granted human beings without an irremediable price being exacted. It is to say that when one watches the innocent suffer (and this woman is innocent), a part of the witness is reminded of, and compares the proximate predicament to, the ultimate visage of all human pain, the archetypal first pain. And I know that to watch her needlessly suffer is not the same in proportion or magnitude, but it evokes an identical emotion from the onlooker, and this pain is too real to negate the emotion surging within.

A thought comes to mind: "In the ordeal of love, there is never just one sufferer; they always come in tandem. There is the suffering the woman experiences, and the consequent pain of the one who must watch her languish."

I touch her in an effort to console, but she does not feel me. I tell her it will be okay, but she does not hear me. I beg, plead, implore her to look at me and share what is wrong, but she does not see me. This moment, like a scratched record playing the same line, repeats itself. I am constantly going to her side, kneeling, touching her with my hand, telling her it will be okay, begging, pleading, imploring, but to no avail. Each time the moment repeats itself, it is a different woman lying upon the bed, but, each time, the emotive qualities evoked are the same. How long this has gone on, I do not know.

Most nights, the vision proceeds no further. It replays without variation. Some nights, the scratched record stops skipping and the moment comes again when the first—the dark-haired woman—reappears on the bed. She is still crying when the door opens and her mother rushes in. I step aside and tell her mother I do not know what is wrong with her daughter. Her mother sidles past me, sits on the bed, and caresses her hands over her daughter's forehead, through her hair, and across her back, all the while whispering soothing words. I am forced, helpless, to stand and watch her daughter's bereavement. I wish to take her pain. If it were mine, I could live with it, could expiate it, but to watch the most innocent and beautiful girl suffer causes me an anxiety and hurt more acute than damnation's fire ever could ignite. It is this agony, I know, this unquenchable agony, I must overcome. But, there is no way to overcome it. My anxiety for her, the overwhelming wish to tell the dream's young woman that everything will be okay, yet not knowing if it will, and knowing she cannot hear or see me: This, this has become my hell—my utter helplessness.

On the nights I experience this part of the dream, I wake sweating and with a bellicose inclination to lash out at whatever invisible demon might still hover over me. I go to the toilet, nauseated, and vomit. I wish the memory of the dream would flush from my system, but it never does. The lingering thought that always haunts me is: If this is the price of love, then I am positive I want nothing to do with it. And I hope in desperation a girl like the one in my dreams does not exist, and, if she does, I hope to never encounter her, not because I would not love her, but because I would love her, and there would always be the chance I might hurt her. How could I live with myself, if I hurt her?

VI

The flash of light departed once more, leaving the creature dumbfounded and overwhelmed by the vividness of its dreams and by the amount of physical exertion required to decipher them. The creature pondered the meaning of the light's unraveling, and of the man's current predicament. *The man lived with two dreams, and they seemed to create two fears,* thought the creature. One was the fear of failing to act, which fashioned him a victim, and the other was the fear of the consequences of his actions, which victimized the innocent. Which path should the man take? And, if he should misstep while upon his chosen path, how far would he be led toward the wrong path? These were not hypotheses one could arbitrarily play out. To test any path required action, but implicit was consequence, and the man feared the consequences of his actions. While the middle-aged man contemplated which path to take, his life passed without him making a decision, and that, too, caused him panic, and during his current confusion, the creature had wandered into his life and sat, now, on the bean that sat on the table.

The creature pitied the poor man. *What strange dreams he suffered,* it thought. And as it watched him slurp his cold soup, it noticed the tangible but slower light again begin its descent. The light curled around the man's cranium and then wafted its way toward the creature. Once again, the light elaborated on the man's waking dream:

The boy, with shallow dips of his spoon, picks up one or two letters at a time. Gone are the moments of puerile exhilaration when he thought of his mother by his side and the full bowl of steaming soup. In their stead is worry, stemming from the moment's fleetingness. He wonders why it did not last.

The boy continues eating, no longer looking up to see his mother's face. He is afraid that even she, the most understanding and compassionate of souls, might not fathom that his happiness diminishes at the same rate as the letters in the soup. The boy dips his spoon into the tomato paste and twirls it around, watching the remaining letters get caught in the undertow that is created by the empty space of the spoon's forward motion. The boy stares into his soup and counts the last letters. Nine. He can afford to, so he begins picking them off one at a time. He dips his spoon into the paste, lifts it, and allows the teetering letters to fall off the spoon, then, with reluctance, swallows only the remaining letter. With four letters left, the boy reluctantly tires and does not wish to complete his ritual.

He stares at the final four letters. The "V" had always been one of his favorites. He liked the way it looked and sounded. He watches as it is dipped under the red paste and its buoyancy causes it to resurge. The boy lets the "V" bounce and make its way toward the edge of the bowl. He turns his attention to the "L" scooting toward the middle. The boy had always been ambivalent of the "L." He liked the look of it when it was capitalized, but saw it lowercase as a simple line, or in cursive as an inadvertent swoosh. The boy places the edge of his spoon at a right angle on the inside of the "L" and drags it in circles, creating a formidable wake. Once the wake abates, the boy turns his attention to the letter "E." He never did like the sound of "E," but did like the look of it. Beside "X," the boy thought "E" aesthetically superior to all other letters. He places his spoon under the letter and raises his spoon halfway from the soup, and then lowers it.

While the gentle light unspooled the man's waking dream, another flash of the same light the creature had felt earlier hit.

"It's a lie," the flash of light announced, its force knocking the creature over. Every flash zapped more energy from the creature, and, after so many bursts, the totality of shocks left the flaccid creature scrambling to regain its bearings. Once composed, the creature hopped back onto the bean and searched for the light, and although it dreaded another flash, the creature needed to know the conclusion of the man's embellished waking dream. Sure enough, the torpid light still wafted from the man, and, once the creature located the light, it recovered the thread.

The boy turns his attention to the final unexamined letter, the "I." He watches it reel to and fro when he moves his spoon up and down. He dunks the "I" under the paste and observes as it exhibits the same buoyancy as the "V." He has surveyed the final four letters and must now perform the inevitable task of finishing his soup.

He closes his eyes and scoops through the paste. He lifts his spoon from the depths. The spoon holds no letters, and the boy is agitated by his failed attempt. He corrals the letters to one side of the bowl to increase his odds, and then re-attempts snatching at one of the four letters. Success! The spoon has picked up the "E" and the "L," and, although he was hoping to devour them one at a time, he knows his ritual does not allow for one of the letters to be put back. At this point in the game, all transactions are final. The boy takes the letters in his mouth and devours them without thought.

He plunks his spoon back into the soup and looks down with remorse at the remaining "V" and "I." He knows once they are gone he will have to return to his banal, empty, real life. The boy raises the spoon from the soup and allows it to fall heavily back. The letters scatter and rock until the soup calms. Once the letters stop moving, the boy closes his eyes and swirls the spoon around so both letters will have an equal chance to find their way into his mouth. The boy then lifts the spoon. He opens his eyes just in time to see he has both letters, but the slight tilt of the spoon along with the thick paste slowly trickling off it edge claims the "I."

The boy devours the "V," and then looks back at the lonely "I" as it careens back and forth, the only letter left to fill the void of tomato paste. The boy is about to finish his game; he knows beyond refutation his moment of bliss has come to an end. He is somber. He lifts his head from the soup and glances to see if his mother is still watching. He is hoping for her reassurance, but as his eyes focus on the place where his mother once stood, they locate nothing but shallow emptiness. She has abandoned him. Perhaps, he thinks, he has taken too long to eat the soup, and her duties called her away. The cause does not matter; to a young boy, desertion is desertion, and the universe is empty when a mother is a single room away.

The boy decides he had better finish the soup. No sense in upsetting his disappearing mother by not at least being thankful for the meal she prepared. He looks down and stares at the lonely "I" engulfed by a thick ocean of tomato paste. The boy, with his eyes wide open, pushes his spoon under the "I" and lifts it into his mouth. He places the "I" between his teeth, but before he devours the letter, looks back into the empty bowl of tomato paste. He thinks, for a moment, about all the letters that had been in the bowl and how empty it now seems, and he begins chewing, almost with anger, masticating the final letter with force. As he does, he thinks to himself how hunger, how the base appetite—after everything else is gone—is the only thing that survives the malaise of life. He thinks of his condition, of his disappointment, and he thinks how often words fail to explain. He looks into the tomato paste void. The boy is old now, and speaks sardonically into his bowl, "Some things cannot be explained by the word, only by its absence."

Then, the light is gone. It offers the creature no explanation, no warning; the torpid light simply vanishes.

VII

The creature sat on the tepid bean and wondered what the latest revelation regarding the man's life might signify. It did not have time to mull over the revelation because the man lurched forward—he was now definitely awake—and grabbed his half-eaten bowl of cold bean soup, and, yelling at the creature, exclaimed, "What is left? What is left to sacrifice? All I have are lies."

Cupping the bowl with both hands, the man screamed in a manner similar to the electric light, "It's all lies. It's all lies. You're a lie!"

Grasping the bowl in his right hand, he flung it as hard as he could over the creature's cowering head, hitting the barren wall.

The bowl ricocheted and scattered shards of glass and beans in every direction. The thick broth dripped down the wall in rivulets patterned after exigent slithering snakes with small translucent copper heads. Only when the shards of glass stopped tumbling, and the man stopped yelling at the blameless creature, during the halcyon aftermath, did the man realize what he had done. To unbridle fiery passion was, to him, altogether foreign and abstract, and perhaps is why it was the man, and not the creature, who shocked himself into action.

He rose from his wobbly chair and started to clean the mess. He paid no mind to the shards of glass embedding themselves into the hard crust and doughy parts of his feet. The man appeared altogether distracted. His action had somehow unraveled him and a trembling fear now seemed to grip his very being. While instinct took over the physical aspect of life, and the man knew the only physical reparation necessary was to clean the mess and erase the evidence of such impetuousness, the mental, the imprinted ethical functions of the mind, began to hound him for his behavior. Why couldn't he, for once, just act, give in to his pent-up anger, dash it upon the wall and watch it run like the way the soup rushed to its final moments and now lay quiet, as a stain. So, too, his anger would run if he could simply uncork it. Such overabundance, such exuberant rebellion, was not, for him, an option. He had trained his mind and heart to suppress such feelings, to quell the vicious storm, and, in an act of self-flagellation, force the pent-up anger deep into his gall, to his guts, where it would writhe and churn in astringent bile, all the while plotting with viciousness the time when it could perhaps surge and rise from his gut to take over the tired man, as it just had.

The man wiped the wall with a wet washrag. He swept the broken glass into a dustpan. The entire time he cleaned up the mess, he never stopped begging aloud for forgiveness. Something peculiar occurred, however: Before he discarded the mess into the trashcan, he stopped, dustpan in hand, and looked for a moment at the wall, toward the very spot the stain had recently besmirched. The creature felt positive the middle-aged man was contemplating throwing down the dustpan. The man stopped asking for forgiveness. The creature could almost feel the moment's impetus; it knew the man to be teetering between some earlier resolution and this new crisis. The moment had become a squeaky fulcrum. The man was tired of something—this, the creature could sense—*but what he was going to do*, the creature pondered.

The man, too, wondered, as he paused in attending to his duties and contemplated throwing down the dustpan as an unapologizing act for allowing his anger to take hold of him. He contemplated the repudiation of his past years' humble and righteous deeds. How had they rewarded him? What had he gained from not allowing his passions to take him over, from not being swayed by the ribald, the indulgent, and the excessive behavior so many had given in to? He was thinking about the total negation of such behavior because the supernal reward he had received for all of his striving to please the overpowering part of his mind was a cold absence of self, an inability to decide on a course of action, a lethargic will to initiate any type of idea that might not align with his current standards, and a bitter resentment toward anything that might not reflect his metallic sense of conscience. His moment of silent contemplation evaporated as quickly as it had come, like an effervescent puff of smoke on a windy day. And then something familiar, reliant—the good old punishing and flagellating part of his brain—took over the man, and he regained composure and his usual sensibilities, remembered what he was doing, and went to the trashcan to throw away the shards of broken glass and filth-covered beans, the reminder of his sullied self, and, as he did so, returned to the appeasing inflections of begging for forgiveness.

After mopping up, the man sat back in his wobbly chair, propped his elbows on the table, and rubbed the back of his head. When he looked up, his eyes were tired and haggard, like someone who has given in to a force both incomprehensible and all-too powerful with which to be reckoned. His tired eyes looked upon the docile creature and pleaded without as much as a needless word. But then the words came anyway, arrived in droves: Pathetic words seeking forgiveness. The man pleaded with the creature. He pleaded until he grew tired of begging, and then sat with his tired head in his hands and started to weep like a child.

The creature was not familiar with this type of suffering. It hadn't thought about it for some time, but wondered whether the old man's story, his ploy to dig to the bottom of suffering and find the light, would help the man. *No*, it thought to itself, in this case it did not have an answer for the middle-aged man. *It is the light, not the darkness, that seeks to punish this man*, thought the creature. It is the light, the light that furled from the man and zapped the creature like an electrical spark. It is this man's tragic quest to only heed the light that is causing such precise pain. Absence of light did not torture the man. The possibility that the source of light was there racked his mind with torment.

The man gathered himself and left the table for the open window. A slight breeze rustled the half-opened blinds, and the moon's stolen light slanted into the room. The creature followed him, perching on his craggy shoulder. The man turned, and, illumined by the quiet light, spoke.

"What does one do to make it through this world, moth? I envy the simple choices you must make. Where and what to eat? Where and when to mate? Where and how to die? Nothing else."

If only it were that easy, thought the creature, but it knew the man did not understand the anxieties it confronted daily. The man went back to the table and sat with his head resting on his clasped hands. Through his fingers, he murmured, "Small moments are the stratum upon which we construct our lives. But, is it ever clear which moment will shatter the entire structure? Or, is it ever really specified: Is there a protocol for how one should act when upon us such moments fall?"

The man was talking, under his breath, to himself. The creature grew reluctant to stay. It couldn't help the man, and to stay any longer was to get carried away with the man's stupor of thought and action. The creature knew its life to be too short-lived not to act. An innate force compelled it to leave. It flew in front of the man's face and tried one final time to thrust out some word, if even a lowly *goodbye*, but all the man heard was the trilling of its wings. He watched the creature float in front of his face and followed it with his gaze as it ventured toward the open window. Although the man had time, and the thought entered his head to close the window so his guest would be forced to stay the night with him, he feared that such action was not acceptable, and, so, instead, he murmured to the creature the word "live" over and over. Much to his chagrin, he watched as the creature, with its drumming wings, exited his open window and his stagnant life.

Swiss Cheese and the Never-Ending Math Equation

OVER the next few weeks, the creature's vivacity began to wane. A brittleness reminiscent of a desiccated and already fallen leaf developed within its frangible wings, attacking the very flow of lifeblood with stasis and pocking the skein of veins with clumps of coagulated blood. The proud and easy beats of the once-vibrant wings came now at a much more belabored cost, and the creature fatigued flying from limb to limb or windowsill to windowsill in spurts it would once have accomplished with ease. This enervation was not confined strictly to its wings. It ran throughout the creature's abdomen, slaking its desire for appetite; it coursed through its heart, causing heavy and almost shatterable beats of overworked muscle; it streamed through its head, masking thoughts with a melancholic mist; it even flooded its antennae, blunting the ability to decipher pure light.

Only wisps of light would reach the creature, and even these came sporadically and without the same fulgor. The creature knew beyond a doubt this loss of light was not a ruse, not some test to overcome in order to attain a more abundant life. It knew, and felt—much in the way the arthritic can recognize the barometric shift in their bones long before an ominous storm arrives—that death fast approached. The creature acquainted itself with the certainty that this stage would be its last, and it accepted its fate with equanimity and not the slightest fear. Almost overnight, its overwhelming need to share the old man's story with the deaf world had dissipated. Gone, too, were the desire to speak and to decipher encountered light.

For the first time in its brief life, the creature contented itself with serving as a corpuscular part of the world's meaningless puzzle. It loved to fill its time with reminiscing about its retrogressive journey. How, in reality, it sought only to return to where it started. Now, it realized the journey itself might have been of more import, as it had created experience. The creature placed value on everything it had learned, but the philosophies of men no longer appealed, and it could not help but notice that even hard-earned lessons melt away like dross and the only thing that remains important is the sterling conviction, the auriferous drive that unnecessary desires and misplaced ambitions spring upon a truth-seeking, naïve heart. In lieu of such a view, the creature believed the process of becoming required appreciation, not the end result of what it had become, nor the pieces of information picked up along the way. Such thinking allowed the creature to no longer worry about its point of view or the views of others. It loved to bask in the light it could not decipher, to feel its mysterious warmth—that was all.

The creature knew if one were to measure in terms of good or bad or through means and ends, its life could be categorized as a disappointment. It had not converted nor managed to assist one soul hold on a little longer by sharing the old man's story. However, the creature did not view its journey with remorse, or as a complete loss; it only wished it had been more involved in living and not so detached. Up until this point, the creature had observed life, even attempted to predict its meaning, without actually experiencing anything of its real heartache. The creature thought how unsympathetic it had been to those who struggled, and it thought how abstract the old man's plight might seem to those who do not know from where their next meal is going to come. It muttered to itself, "All this time seeing, yet not, and all this time hearing, yet not. I have been blind and deaf to the cares of the world."

This type of thinking would cause the creature to struggle in the deep cesspool of self-pity and self-doubt, but, then, like always, it would grasp hold of that trusty old life raft—hope—or it would cling to the final thread of some invisible notion of faith in the anticipated reward and release itself from the pit of despair, rise from the dark ocean of doubt it had again splashed into, and it would remember how dear the old man's unreachable ideals were, how meaningful they made its life, and it would long to be back in his secure presence.

This final thought caused the creature to slowly, and without an actual plotted course, meander its way to the old man. It experienced the prescient feeling that it would never make the journey back alive, but it knew it must try. When the creature first left the middle-aged man's house, it had a distinct impression and a desire to simply fly as fast as it could, anywhere. It had flown for weeks without noting in which direction it fluttered, but now that it was necessary to return to its birthing place, an innate compass housed inside most creatures and children recalled the general direction, and, so, the creature zigzagged its line due west.

Along the way, cognizant for the first time of typical wants and needs, the creature began to experience the common pangs of hunger, coldness, fatigue, and melancholy, all of which were ever-present on its journey, but, up to this point, kept in check by the more pressing desire to share the old man's story. It pleased the creature to experience these prosaic emotions and hackneyed burdens of being. In extremity, it now knew it lived. True, the creature had seen its fair share of trials, but it was always able to pass them off as simple obstacles placed along the road, or as stumbling blocks enabling it to grow. Once the creature lost sight of any higher meaning in its life, these experiences affected it like they do the common person—deflection became impossible. This awareness of its awful plight caused the creature to stir with an emotion akin to love of one's brother. Now, it would enter doorways, windows, and open flues, and perch undetected in a veiled corner to observe humanity in its most ordinary surroundings and at work on the most menial of tasks, content to bask unnoticed in the golden glow of the unfiltered and sweaty stench. One day, while recuperating from a short flight, the creature happened to enter the shattered window of a big building near a sign with a neon glow.

Upon entering the large room, the creature noticed the place abuzz with activity. The description of the location need not be explicated. It noted the aisles and rows of seats, the giant stage veiled by a plush, velvety curtain running to the ceiling, the precisely situated lighting—a feature all moths can appreciate—casting a surreal glow on the curtain, and little else. The auditorium filled with voices and people coming and going, some fidgeting, some popping their heads from behind the curtain the way a mole cautiously exits its mound to espy danger. In the center of all this confusion and preparation sat one man, about halfway back in the middle section of the seating. The man was tended to by what looked like three assistants: A woman on his right with a clipboard in hand, and two men to his left also holding clipboards. The man was telling the three assistants something, and it must have been important because all were leaning toward him, stalwarts listening to each word, then jotting things down. The creature could not help but think how they looked like needy sunflowers straining to absorb the sun's expedient and effulgent rays.

After the man said whatever it was he said, the woman immediately withdrew from the others and walked behind the curtain through a small entrance just left of the stage. The creature watched as the woman, after a moment, reappeared and descended the same small staircase, walking back to the man's side. She whispered something into his ear and then stood up straight, turning to the stage. All four were now facing the stage as if some expectant guest were to momentarily make an appearance. The creature noticed a hush prevail throughout the auditorium. The man sitting in the middle, surrounded by his assistants, suddenly yelled, "Lights."

The backlighting dimmed and the lights pointed directly over the stage burned brighter With the onset of darkness, the auditorium grew still and silent. All eyes were directed at the curtain, which retracted squeakily to unveil on stage a peculiar slab of something. The creature did not know what it was, sitting moored like an enormous ship and featuring gigantic holes too large for regular port holes, and too randomly placed to create a recognizable pattern. The enormous dull slab was colored a pearly off-white, only dirtier, and with a tinge of brown and yellow around the edges and holes. Leading to three of the holes were three enormous contraptions resembling scaffolding, only they were retractable and could be raised higher or lower, and they included steps straddling the slide that ran down the scaffolding and almost to the stage's edge. At the bottom of each slide sat what appeared to be three of the largest corks ever constructed. Near the edge of the stage, a pile of agglomerated cork granules large enough to comprise roughly three more corks sat inert. On top of the pile teetered a long two-man saw.

The entire scene loomed even more peculiar because on stage, to the left and right of the behemoth thing, a motley crew stared up at it like it was a spaceship arrived from another planet. This strange cast of characters consisted of what looked like ancient prophets and peoples drawn directly from the Bible. Some of the cast appeared to have come from Greek tragedy, and some from eighteenth-century novels. There were others that looked like musicians. One carried a guitar, another a miniature piano, and one held a harmonica. Some looked like they had been ripped straight from the pages of storied fables, including three large mice that wore glasses and carried canes and seemed to be salivating. Still others among the cast, the creature could not even venture a guess as to what they might be. They stood, most with their hands placed on their hips, and all with their necks kinked upward (except for the mice and one blind man) to behold the immense hunk filling the stage. The man directing the scene stood—the creature could see only his outline—and with a proud voice and arms upraised, bellowed: "Ladies and gentleman, I give you: 'Swiss Cheese and the Never-Ending Math Equation.'"

The crowd of workers, scattered sparsely in the seats and those gawking on stage, clapped with excitement. The man, who still stood with arms lifted, lowered them and stared at his creation. "In five minutes, rehearsals will commence," he yelled into his megaphone.

And with this, he dismissed all who stared at the slab of cheese. The lights were flipped back on, and the purple curtain once again slid over to veil the stage. The creature was glued to its corner. The strange man and peculiar cast of characters caused it to stir with frantic emotion. It knew the entertainment value of watching such a peculiar act unfold would be worth its time.

Immediately after the five-minute signal was announced and the lights turned back on, the female assistant began to anxiously stir. This would be her fourth play as the man's understudy, the previous three smashing successes, but she felt he had gone too far this time, and considered the theme a bit pedantic, or, better yet, a bit crazy, but how could she feather such a premonition to the man without hurting his feelings or seeming conceited. "Sir," she began in a voice quieter and more acquiescent than retreating mouse feet. "Sir," she said again, this time with a little more emphasis.

The director turned his head her way. "What is it, my dear? Do you have something to say?"

She knew the time for thought had passed, and, now, hopefully, reflex and action would prove the correct course. "Well, yes sir. Actually, I do have something on my mind."

"Well, out with it, my dear; let's hear what troubles you."

The woman began, the director and his two male attendants staring into her confident yet apologetic face. "Well, sir, I just think it seems strange for a play to have a giant chunk of Swiss cheese with ten holes and only nine corks to plug them. I find it unsettling, among other things, that you wish to keep that chunk of uncut cork on stage and in the way. Seeing how you will always be one cork short, why not cut the tenth before the play begins?"

The woman did not eschew the actual subject. She felt the truth, as brutal as it might be, would be better, and, for the director, it was. For so long, he had dealt with people who thought him a genius and were afraid to question anything he did; it was true, at times, he would produce the most abstract, meaningless plays simply to see if he could get away with it, and many times he not only got away with it, but the cronies would actually compliment his bold and daring moves and attribute to them truth or beauty far beyond his actual intentions. However, his current play was not an exercise in abstraction, and it was somewhat dear to him and fraught with parabolic significance, so he proceeded to explain to the woman his intent.

"I thank you for being so brutally upfront with me, my dear. I find it refreshing that some people still question the validity of certain acts. And, so, let me explain. There are nine corks. And there are ten holes that will be filled with actors in their corresponding places. Once the eight corks are in place, which must be achieved before the rehearsal begins, the ninth hole will be plugged during the play. This will leave a single hole always empty. In the open hole, under the shining light, each actor will voice his part of the tale, but, before finishing, the man who pushes the corks will put the cork, taken from another hole, into place, cutting off the actors mid-sentence, and the lights will then move to the vacant hole. The same process will continue over and again. Aside from the beginning, where two holes will appear void but only one will bask in the limelight, there will always be a hole that undergoes unplugging to plug another hole. This process will continue until the curtain is drawn."

The man continued, in flurried excitement, to reveal his design. "In this play, there isn't an end, per se, but a crashing of the curtain on a drama that is not meant to be performed. The crux, the play's basis—and understand, it is rife with symbolic meaning—is that the action continues to circumvent, and, each time a hole is plugged, another one is always created; there is no end. Of course, if there were time, and perhaps if the man who plugs the holes with cork, or even if the crew who moves the scaffolding would stop moving it and instead construct the last cork out of the ample material set on stage, then perhaps the possibility would exist to plug all ten holes, but they are so occupied—and this is the point—in plugging the current hole that there is no time to construct the tenth cork. Now, my dear, I know the premise seems crazy and I know it is complex, and so much of the play hinges on a metaphysical notion that to the common person seems like a ridiculous play from a deranged director, but, I assure you, meaning is present."

And, with his last comment, the director winked at the woman in hopes she understood. Meanwhile, the other two assistants clapped a roaring ovation and stuttered, "Oh, how brilliant. How absolutely marvelous. When will the common man recognize his brilliance?" The director turned a cold shoulder on such lavish praise and continued to look at the woman.

She could approbate the block of cork with the two-man saw now on it, and, to illustrate, nodded her assent when the director winked, but she still did not understand why the scaffolding had to be lowered or raised from hole to hole by the emaciated Caucasian people in bondage being taunted with whips and lashes by darker and rather ferocious-looking taskmasters, nor did she understand why a piece of cheese was the choice for this strange re-enactment. *Couldn't the director simply have used nine doors,* she wondered. And, so, since he answered her first question in a peaceful manner, the woman grew brazen and asked her other questions. And, once again, the director was grateful for his assistant's directness, and was happy to explain his intentions.

"Now, keep in mind this is a contemporary play, and these are contemporary times, and even though the old notion of symbols and archetypes has proven to fail us time and again, we still cling to it, and I assure you symbols are an integral part of my play's meaning," he offered. "The people in bondage highlight the deprived depths and unwillingness of the entire process; they must be forced to work. Of course, there are other reasons to use them, but this explanation should suffice. And the cheese is used because, well, quite frankly, I liked the idea. I suppose you could say it is used to illustrate the ephemeral notion of life and upon what shaky ground the very myth and structure is founded, but I prefer to use this food because after a few weeks the whole firmament that started out smelling so good turns rotten and stinks, and putrescence is an integral part of this play."

The two assistants were clapping again and sharing comments meant to be overheard: "Oh, the ingenuity of our director. Who else would think of cheese, of cheese?"

Only after the director's stern "enough" did they cease their ostentatious praise. In fairness, however, there is always a place in this world for such satellites. One rarely grows tired of praise, even unwarranted. "Enough of this," said the man. "Don't you know that too much meaning kills meaning? Just sit back and watch the play unfold."

The woman knew when to answer with silence, and, so, she said no more, but deep inside still harbored numerous questions and wondered if the director hadn't perhaps crossed the line of good art and delved into material she termed "too abstract."

The director helped the woman to her seat by taking her arm and politely escorting her. Then, he sat down, but not before one of his assistants fluffed and placed a pillow upon the seat. When the man lowered himself, he turned once more to the woman. Of all his assistants throughout the years, none had been as reliable in judgment, and, at the moment, her troubles worried him. "Did you know," he whispered ambivalently. "Did you know, the larger the hole, the higher the quality of cheese? It is as if the bacteria's great absence is responsible for infusing what is left with such rife flavor. Think about it."

The woman nodded and was about to consider his supposition, but the lights were again fading, the curtain was opening, the actors had assumed their positions, and the director yelled into his megaphone, "Commence in five, four, three, two, one..."

Swiss Cheese and the Never-Ending Math Equation

(The curtain is drawn. To begin, eight corks are in place and covering the holes. Two holes remain open. One opening features three heads looking out, and three more in the

background trying to see beyond the first three. The taskmasters are whipping the slaves as they turn the handle to raise the scaffolding toward the vacant hole. The man who pushes the cork into place sits on one, and, with interest, watches. The outer lights dim, and the limelight is directed toward the hole and the three men.)

Dead Novelist #1[1]:

Why, the way those masters wield the whip and flaunt power over those
poor slaves takes me back to the atrocious maritime floggings.
Such malfeasance is always the case when authority is conferred
and its sister virtue, wisdom, is absent.

Dead Novelist #2:

The right to adjudication and authority are one and the same, yet how
can one simply say that this person is worthy of this, or that
person is worthy of that, when self is a vague and abstract
expression that creates a reality which may or may not exist
outside historical realms, and, if it does exist, is different for each
person, and, therefore, when laws are predicated upon a
standard so abstract and independent of a collective
consciousness they are really instituted for the good of the few
that divvy out the judgment, and not for those who stand at the
other end of that cold gavel in the first place.

Living Author:

And, yet, without authority, anarchy would prevail.

First Critic of the Living Author:

(From the background) What the author is saying is that without the concept
of authority, or without the fear of law, there would be nothing
to keep appetite in check.

Second Critic of the Living Author:

(From the background) What the first critic misunderstands when he
interprets the living author is that what would actually prevail
without authority would be survival of the fittest, which is not

---

[1] It is not the author's intent to replicate specific persons. If the dominate voice is similar to an actual author or musician, it is simply because that voice dominated the zeitgeist of the specific era and/or the present era. All characters in the novelist and musician sections are archetypes of their time period, and should be regarded as such.

appetite but a biological function that keeps order and is not
lawlessness but rather the ultimate law: Nature.

Third-Year Graduate Student:

(From the background) What Critics One and Two proclaim is that the
author does not actually mean anarchy, per se; for lack of a
better term, the author references this one without fully
appreciating the implications.

Dead Novelist #1:

Hold the anchor a moment! When did deckhands find it wise to abandon
the mizzen mast and put words in the captain's mouth?

Living Author:

Ah, my friend. It's been quite a spell since you have written. The market,
these days, is saturated with critics. There are critics for all a
novel's facets. Critics write the foreword, afterword, biographical
sketch, and the newest trend is for the critic to highlight, for the
reader, the novel's shortcomings. Critics supply the text its
meaning. It is best to consider what a critic says about a novel,
rather than read the book yourself. One day, we shall read only
Cliff's Notes.

Dead Novelist #1:

I never had a stomach for such parasites. They are like mosquitoes that,
upon sucking the minutest portion of blood from a miniscule
vein, proclaim, like synecdoche, to understand the entire
measure of man: Width, breadth, and depth.

Living Author:

Well, be that as it may, the world is full of mosquitoes and to write
nowadays requires a novelist's skin to make an elephant's look as
smooth as a baby's bottom.

Dead Novelist #2:

(Not allowing the critics time to speak) One must repudiate such institutions
that exonerate the critic and trample the artist. While the artist
seeks to build something, the critic destroys, knocking down
walls he did not erect, doling out opinions like the sprinkler head
disperses filthy water—of course, some seeds will sprout, but
most are submerged in the excess of words and carried away
with the runoff—and, if destruction is not enough, we allow

them to sit in judgment over us; we allow someone who has suffered neither the artist's pangs nor intensity, someone who would refuse to starve for a measly meal, someone who would refuse to spend agonizing nights struggling to remember a thought, the one too brilliant for words, for, if it were put into words, it would shrivel on the page because some thoughts are ever-expanding and can't be contained nor defined; like a beam of light, they come and go so rapidly that all that remains is the dull impression or the streak that is still imprinted on our minds, and we say, *here, Mr. Critic, here you go, here is the sledgehammer and here is the glass house I have spent five years of my life constructing; now, swing mighty Mr. Critic, because there is a line of critics behind you waiting, so you only get one swing. Never mind I still live in the house, Mr. Critic; I can always construct another one, right?* But it isn't the house they wish to examine and destroy. No, it is the artist himself. They set the breathing body of your work, or the biographical background that is none of their business and held sacred to the author, on a cold metal table and shine light into its anesthetized eyes and tell it not to wince as they dissect its serous veins and not to cringe as its essence spatters all over. It is only ink veins dissecting, there is nothing human, and therefore irreplaceable, underneath all that paper flesh—and so we allow them this kind of authority because we know art and the artist are not subject to a critic's blunt scalpel, because the creator never asks the creation if it validates him, because water and fire are elementally disparate and will never suffuse into one cohesive elemental…

Dead Novelist #1:

My friend, I do not mean to cut you off, but for a second I recognized the simulacrum of a megalomaniac I once created. I would advise, if I were not so invigorated by the spirit of your beliefs, that you pace yourself. We old men cannot keep up with the rising generation's anger and intensity.

Dead Novelist #2:

The rising generation has crested—it pinnacled in 1861 and again in 1914, and yet again in 1939, and in its nadir has crashed upon the shore and scurried back to the ocean to regain fury, only to crash again upon itself. So rises and falls the constant tide of history. History is a whore and mankind its illegitimate child. History is the eternal thrust of a bloody spearhead and the socio-political platform, the hand that twists the point ever deeper into the vitals. History is created and destroyed in the same moment, and the aftermath, the callow wish to return, carries through the centuries the cross of mankind.

Living Author:

Ah, yes. The absentmindedness of history never ceases to amaze. History is a dog that returns to   his own vomit.

First Critic:

It is important to note the Author uses the possessive pronoun "his," instead of the androgynous pronoun "it." This usage implies that "man" in his rudimentary and fallen state is the dog that returns to his vomit, which in this case signifies war.

Second Critic:

The first critic insightfully points out the particular pronoun that disrupts and adds meaning to the sentence, but also important to note is the derogatory tone of the entire sentence, which in essence states that man does not have the capacity to learn from others' mistakes and must experience them firsthand.

Third-Year Graduate Student:

Critics One and Two allude to the nihilistic nature of the Living Author, and it is these remarks, coupled with the Living Author's earlier remark, that alerts us he has a true disdain for man and life.

(The extended scaffolding is raised by the slaves so the slide lines up with the hole. The loose cork sits in place at the slide's bottom. The man who slides the cork is about to shoulder the heavy load (about 3.9 pounds) up the slide, which he straddles by using the stairs located to either side.)

Dead Novelist #1:

Now, enough is enough. Who is this third person commenting on what these two numbskulls have said?

Living Author:

Why, he is a graduate student, studying my life for his dissertation.

Dead Novelist #1:

Well! Why is it, then, that he will not directly quote you? And how is it
that his information, from what you have actually said, seems so
skewed?

Living Author:

(*Chuckling*) Oh my, how strange this second-hand account must seem, but
I assure you this is the way of academia these days. A student
cannot come right out just yet and quote me, the primary source.
He must first learn from the critics and reference them as much
as possible, and, then, once he boasts sufficient knowledge, he
may begin formulating his own ideas on the subject.

Dead Novelist #1:

And seven years of schooling is not enough time in which to formulate an
idea? Ideas are not bred in molasses!

Dead Novelist #2:

It is, once again, a question of authority and existence. A student does not
exist, nor may he flaunt authority, until he has been published.
Only then does he exist, and only then does he no longer answer
to others. Quite a conundrum the university has created.

Living Author:

Well, unless the student is abnormally bright, eight to ten years is about
the right period of time during which to keep on the training
wheels.

Dead Novelist #1:

And you don't grow tired of all the petty and erroneous criticism?

Living Author:

One learns to accept all things.

Dead Novelist #1:

Not I. I can never accept such things.

Living Author:

You would not make it in my century.

Dead Novelist #1:

Nor would I want to. My century was bleak enough without surrender.

Living Author:

Your century's cloud of bleakness has led to my century's interminable
storm of depression.

Dead Novelist #1:

Oh, yes, even back then I peered into the soul of man with a periscope, and, from a distance, I witnessed the future's impending doom. It was, and ever will be, the improper use of authority. The few who lead the many astray, be it from a social, political, economic, or even religious platform.

Living Author:

Religion is the poster child for blatant exploitation.

Dead Novelist #1:

And, suppose, not to switch the subject if you wish to continue spinning yarn in this direction, but, suppose I ask this graduate student a question, can he provide his own answer, or will he regurgitate a critic's phrase?

Living Author:

Depends on the student. Ask him a question.

Dead Novelist #1:

Why, yes, I suppose I will. You there! Have you a thought of your own?

Third-Year Graduate Student:

Yes, sir, I have.

Dead Novelist #1:

And what, my good young man, is occupying your skull?

Third-Year Graduate Student:

You mean right this second?

Dead Novelist #1:

Why, I surely do not mean later.

Third-Year Graduate Student:

(*Stuttering*) I, I, I don't know. I wasn't really thinking right now about anything.

Dead Novelist #1:

What? A blank sheet. Not a single line of thought? No note that strikes you, boy? How about a word? What word comes to mind, if I ask you for one?

Third-Year Graduate Student:

A word, sir? I am not sure I grasp your meaning.

Dead Novelist #1:

My goodness. Seven years and you, my boy, are hardly suitable to serve as an anchor; even it makes a sound when it hits the ocean's bottom. Let me offer you a piece of advice. I am magnanimous and wish to save you some trouble. (*He puts his arm around the student and peers, with him, out the hole. The man who slides the cork is interrupted, breathing profusely and leaning with his back against the cork, about halfway up the slide.*)

Dead Novelist #1:

Look out there! Tell me what you see.

Third-Year Graduate Student:

(*Staring into the blackness*) Nothing at all.

Dead Novelist #1:

That is correct. Embrace the nothingness for a while and come back and tell me what you have found, and I promise you when I ask you for a word, the only difficulty you will have is determining which one best describes nothing.

(*With that, Dead Novelist #1 heaves the boy out the hole and down the slide. The graduate student hits the cork and sends it, along with the man, sliding onto the stage.*)

Dead Novelist #1:

Now, that is how one sets a boy on the correct path. That boy is now educationally initiated.

Living Author:

(*In amazement*) How could you be so cruel? He was simply trying to learn.

Dead Novelist #1:

Exactly. I have done him a service, which is more than I can say for you.

Man Who Slides the Corks:

(*Stands up, rubbing his back. To the director*) I am not paid for this! I nearly broke my back! Any more of this nonsense and I will quit!
(*Director remains silent*)

Dead Novelist #2:

(*Laughing*) Over my lifetime, I don't think I learned to laugh like I am now. That is the way one should dispose of a body. Finally, some elbowroom in this stuffy place.

Dead Novelist #1:

I quite like the close quarters.

Living Author:

I still cannot believe you would treat someone like that!

Dead Novelist #1:

Oh, you sourpuss. He will be fine. Now, stop complaining, or you will be
next.

First Critic:

What the author is expressing is the inhumanity of your behavior, and,
yet, you perform such atrocious acts humanistically.

Dead Novelist #1:

Ah! Humanity! My friend. You have no right to question my motives or
my actions.

First Critic:

I question everything.

Dead Novelist #1:

Yes, I am quite sure of that, and I am also sure that you answer
everything. So, tell me, Mr. Critic, what never stands on its own
two legs, never relies on its own brain, and, as of yet, is incapable
of flight?

First Critic:

Well, now, give me a second.

Dead Novelist #1:

I see, hard to come up with something on your own? Do you need your
muse, the author, to answer it for you, and then you can explain
what he has said?

First Critic:

No, I just need silence for a moment, so I can think. If you wouldn't
mind?

Dead Novelist #1:

Oh, yes, there seems to be a shortage these days of silence. Allow my
good friend to escort you to a peaceful spot.

(Dead Novelist #2 grabs First Critic by the coattails and throws him out the hole.
The critic runs into the cork and the man who slides it, who had, again, started up the
slide.)

Dead Novelist #2:

Well, now, that felt quite good.

Dead Novelist #1:

Yes, it does, doesn't it?

Living Author:

You two should be ashamed of yourselves.

Dead Novelist #2:

We have lived with enough guilt and shame to sink this very continent. It is not like a little more will burden these shoulders.

Dead Novelist #1:

(*Laughing*) How true.

Man Who Slides the Cork:

(*To the director*) I will not work under these conditions! I have said it once and will not tell you again! I am not indestructible. My aching bones cannot bear the brunt of such blows. (*Looking up at the hole*) If there are any additional bodies to be expected, let me know; otherwise, there is going to be a bloody mess when I get up there.

Dead Novelist #1:

Well, in that case, you'd better hold off for another minute, or body— whichever comes first.

Director:

(*Into megaphone*) None of this is in the script. Just stick to your lines and don't improvise.

Dead Novelist #2:

(*Under his breath*) Yet another authoritarian, this one shapeless and loud, like he resides in my head.

Living Author:

I hope, by the way, you were not insinuating that my last critic is also to go. I will not brook such brutish nonsense.

Second Critic:

(*Backing up against the wall*) I, I, I,

Dead Novelist #2:

Do us a favor, you babbling fool, and start all your sentences from now on with a period.

Second Critic:

I, I, I don't know what you mean.

Dead Novelist #2:

Let me explain. You start a sentence like this (.) and it is over before it begins. The reader can immediately stop because they know you have nothing more to say. Start doing it. I don't mind that it was my idea; you have earned it.

Second Critic:

What are you saying?

Dead Novelist #1:

I believe he is saying that with some people it is over before it ever
    began.

(*Dead Novelist #1 grabs second critic's sleeve and tugs him toward the hole. Living
Author grabs his legs and tries to keep the critic inside the hole. Dead Novelist #2
kicks critic in the backside and forces him out. The critic crashes to the stage and runs
off. The man who slides the cork laughs.*)

Living Author:

I am ruined. How could you two be so heartless?

Dead Novelist #1:

I find it comes quite naturally.

Dead Novelist #2:

Yes, with each body it is easier.

Living Author:

What shall I do now? Who will validate me?

Dead Novelist #2:

You mean, without your critics you do not exist? Well, then, I see no
    harm in throwing you out, since a ghost cannot feel pain and
    lacks authority.

(*Dead Novelists #1 and #2 grab the Living Author and throw him out, but, before
doing so, inform the man who slides the cork to move out of the way, which he does.*)

Dead Novelist #1:

(*Metaphorically washing his hands*) Well, now the two of us can sit and
    discuss weightier matters.

Dead Novelist #2:

Indeed. If these men represent the new generation, the world is in trouble.
    These four are like the hollow cloud's pomp, appearing full until
    one comes directly in contact with the thin air.

Director:

(*Into megaphone*) This is not in the script, gentlemen. Stick to the script.

Dead Novelist #2:

Behold, even the non-existent blackness seeks to enforce upon us its
    authority.

Dead Novelist #1:

I look into the very gale of blackness and say *do your worst*. If the whiteness
were to speak to us, I would listen and then would I fear.

Dead Novelist #2:

(*With a look of worry*) The new world is simply the old world parading
around under a different name and in different fashions. Once
man learns to grasp the endless now, he will be on his way to
understanding. Nothing really changes.

Dead Novelist #1:

The endless now; what constitutes such a phenomenon?

Dead Novelist #2:

Let me attempt explanation: If life were a string that stretched infinitely in
two directions and one represented the future and the other the
past and the finger on the string was the present, and you were
to use that finger to pull the string, the ripple would travel in
both directions, affecting the past and the future; then, what is
the past but the current ripple running through it, and what is
the future but the same ripple? All things depend on the now:
The future, the past, and the present are one giant undulation
that continuously runs through our lives, only there are a few
caveats man must discern—that is, he did not pull the string, nor
is the ripple that runs through it *his*, the string is actually one
continuous circle, a rippling uruborus that continues to turn and
twist, and is infinite and cannot change either the end or the
beginning, as these two things that constitute past and future are
determined before death and birth; humans simply experience
the ripple as it purges their lives, mistake it for circumstance and
free will and trial and all the other transitory links that make us
misinterpret life for the conundrum it is—the error lies in
thinking that changing a course of action can actually affect the
ripple; only when man realizes that he is the tail being eaten by
the head, or the head that is eating the tail, can he live in the
endless now, can he recognize the ripple existed before time and
will continue to after time's field ceases to contain.

Dead Novelist #1:

Yes. I have often noted events that shaped who we are and how we think occurred long before the embryo constituting came into being, and will endure long after we are laid to rest.

Dead Novelist #2:

We must stop focusing on time and realize everything, including past and future, is laid before us in the endless now. The past is never behind us and the future is never ahead. It is ever-present.

Dead Novelist #1:

And what will the graduate student see as he tries to feel his way through a world that concerns itself more with time than it does with shades; if he ever returns, what word will his tongue speak?

(*The man sliding the cork nears the top and is about to plug the hole.*)

Dead Novelist #2:

The word. Ah, yes, what single word will he speak? The word that will puncture the eardrums, shake dust from the flesh, and rattle the soul—what word? What word could be screamed so loud it would shatter the very foundation? In times past it was *freedom*, but, now, would agency be revered with so many voluntarily chained?—the word, what is it, is at the very tip of my tongue, the word, what is it? I've got it.

(*The man pushes the cork into place, plugging the hole. Nothing remains but silence. The lights move to another vacant hole, from which three musicians peer out.*)

Modern Musician:

Music, like scent, is the strongest remembrance of time past, time immemorial. Every time I smell human putrescence in empty alleys or subway stations, the impurities take me back to my first thirty years, much like every time I hear the pealing roar of a mad organ as I walk past a sorry church I remember my first ten.

Old Poet/Musician:

Look out, kid. The rising generation will brand you the spokesman for their disbelief, and patent your life as an appendage to their own if you aren't careful. How old are you?

Modern Musician:

Just turned thirty-one.

Old Poet/Musician:

Pessimist?

Modern Musician:

Realist!

Old Poet/Musician:

Of course, time does not measure experience any more than weight
measures loss.

Modern Musician:

Oh, no. If loss weighed, we would all be found at the ocean's bottom;
barnacles clinging to a ship that sank before it ever left the
harbor.

Old Poet/Musician:

Strapped to the anchor labeled *hope*, I am sure. We wouldn't have it any
other way. Happiness' weightless balloon might send one
skyward, but it also blocks their view of the stars. We long for
the action, the energy, of life, not the bypassing thereof.

Modern Musician:

Well, if it takes bitter to make sweet, I can forego both, and if it takes pain
to make beauty, I think I would like to crawl back into the cave
or under the rock.

Old Poet/Musician:

The fall has you afraid of heights.

Modern Musician:

No. The ascent to humanity has me wishing to return to barbarism. We
are still apes. Don't let the suit and tie fool you.

Old Poet/Musician:

Well, I won't be the first to admit that throughout history humans have
demonstrated more wolf than man, have bared the canines more
than the smile, but there is still hope.

Modern Musician:

Optimist! I have heard the modern musician say—and I think he is
generous in his assessment of humanity—that the light in the
hearts of man has gone out. The candle has been smothered by
the bushel.

Old Poet/Musician:

Ah, he must speak of the masses, but he errs, for the candle that lights the
soul was never to be found in the masses.

Modern Musician:

136

Pessimist?

Old Poet/Musician:

Individualist! It won't be long before we return to tribes. The state has
    seen her day in the sun, and now she rots from the inside.

Modern Musician:

They say the loneliest person can be found in a crowd.

Musician #3:

(*Moves slowly toward old poet and places an ear to the man's chest, pauses as if
    listening to his heartbeat, then lifts his head and walks over to Modern
    Musician, repeating the process by lifting his head for a moment and then
    placing his ear back upon the Musician's chest. He looks at the two
    perplexed musicians and smiles, takes a step back, sits at his mini piano,
    and motions for the two to lift their instruments. His fingers lightly tap the
    keys. Piano resounds in syncopation. He looks at the two imploringly, and,
    without a word, invites them to join him. The three play for a time. The
    music introduces harmony. The Old Poet and Modern Musician feel the
    intertwining of notes. Meanwhile, the slaves have lowered the scaffolding into
    position with the hole and the man who slides the cork again begins his
    ascent. The music stops.*)

Man Who Slides the Cork:

(*Clapping, while leaning against the cork, about two-thirds of the way up the slide. He
    then takes the cigarette from his mouth and begins to speak.*) Bravo,
    bravissimo. How I love music without the spoken word. It is the
    grinding axis of the celestial spheres.

Director:

(*Into the megaphone, perturbed*) There are no cigarettes allowed on stage, and
    by no means is this in the script.

Man Who Slides the Cork:

For my meager wages I will do as I please. (*Director leans over to his assistant
    and whispers that they may need a replacement.*)

Director:

(*Into megaphone*) Carry on.

Old Poet/Musician:

Music is its own word and speaks volumes in a million different
    languages. The universal language that ties together so much of
    this world.

Modern Musician:

How often the things that keep us together fall apart. And, then what?

Old Poet/Musician:

We put it back together. Like a kaleidoscope.

Modern Musician:

And when the puzzle pieces don't fit?

Old Poet/Musician:

They will fit. You just need to make a new puzzle.

Modern Musician:

They fit how? Fit like a finger in an eye, or a finger in a light socket?

Old Poet/Musician:

You know, the late doctor assessed correctly that wit is simply anger
turned sideways.

Modern Musician:

And belief is doubt turned soft.

Old Poet/Musician:

Belief is doubt analyzed to the uttermost mite. Don't think existentialism
doesn't attack a Christian in the same manner it attacks an
atheist. Only, the Christian existentialist asks more profoundly
the question of "Why?"

Modern Musician:

They are all neurotics. They should learn not to ask questions, and instead
live. There is no God in all that empty space.

Old Poet/Musician:

In order for your anger and rebellion to be considered valid, it must rise
up against the very God you disregard and trample. In so
vehemently denying God, you accomplish nothing more than
proclaiming your belief. You are like a branch trying to strangle
the very vine that nourishes life.

Modern Musician:

There is no God and there is no Devil. There is no heaven and there is no
hell. Who would need hell when we have ourselves?

Old Poet/Musician:

God or Devil, you have yourself, and that is a weighty matter.

Modern Musician:

Well, anyway, speaking of vines, since you brought them up, I'm just here
for the wine. I saw the superfluous size of those corks and
figured the bottles should be grand enough to drown any
sorrow. But, my, how long this day…

*(The hole is plugged. The light moves to a hole near the bottom left-hand corner of the
cheese. The slaves are whipped toward the scaffolding as they begin to lower it to
position. Inside the hole, three voracious mice nibble, while a blind man silently sits.)*

Mouse #1:

Eat up, old man; tomorrow we may die.

Old Blind Man:

I am not hungry.

Mouse #2:

Shrivel up and die, then. More food for us.

Mouse #3:

Come on, you two, have a little pity on the old man. Can't you see, I
mean, can't you sense that he has been through much.

Mouse #1:

Oh, yes, again with your compassion. "The oldest hath bourne the most.
The oldest hath bourne the most." We know. We grow tired of
such malapropisms. It is the century of appetite, my friend.

Old Blind Man:

I believe you mistake me for another. My hurt runs more ancient and
three times deeper. My banishment is my own curse. I do not
seek pity or understanding, only justice.

Mouse #2:

And, what is more just than an emaciated man who happens to stumble
upon walls made from food?

Old Blind Man:

Death! I have died a thousand deaths, yet cannot settle the score with
Fate.

Mouse #3:

And what, then, is your sin? How have you tempted Fate?

Old Blind Man:

My sin was my ignorance.

Mouse #3:

The ignorant cannot sin.

Old Blind Man:

One upsets the balance by what he does, not by what he knows. Knowing
only accentuates the hurt.

Mouse #1:

You have fasted too long, old man. What you need is to indulge.

Old Blind Man:

Indulgence was another of my sins.

Mouse #2:

Aren't these transgressions, in lieu of sin?

Old Blind Man:

Open rebellion or unintentional rebellion. I perceive no difference.

Mouse #2:

Well, sure there is a difference. One lets you get away without obsessing
on remorse.

Old Blind Man:

We get away with nothing. Don't you understand?

Mouse #2:

You get away with nothing. I will steal your cheese.

Old Blind Man:

I give it voluntarily.

Mouse #1:

Imagine, this guy is on a hunger strike while living within a piece of
cheese. Hah, the gods must not tire of playing with you, my
friend.

*(Just then, a noise is heard. Inch by inch, a cork comes out of place as pounding is
heard on the other side, then it crashes to the stage floor. Another light moves to the hole
and reveals the culprits: Dead Novelists #1 and #2.)*

Dead Novelist #1:

(Yelling) Fellow inmates, these portholes can be knocked out with a good
heave-ho. *Heave!* I say to all those trapped in the bowels of
darkness. *Heave away!*

(A ruckus is discerned as coming from behind some of the other holes.)

Director:

(Into megaphone) Enough is enough. You two are ruining my play. You
don't speak your lines, you talk out of turn, and you have
ruthlessly rid yourselves of the other actors.

Dead Novelist #2:

Actor? I play no part but my own.

(*Two more corks come crashing down. Two more lights are employed to determine what lies behind the holes.*)

Three Railroad Workers:

(*Looking toward the Old Blind Man and the mice*) I believe we have taken on vagrants. (*They spit their wads of chew toward the mice. Their aim is off, and plugs lands on three women gathered below.*)

Fairy Tale Woman #1:

Ew, was that bat dung that just landed on my dress? My stepmother will kill me.

Fairy Tale Woman #2:

Oh, go sleep it off and you'll be fine.

Fairy Tale Woman #3:

You mean to tell me I grew my hair all this time and that idiot director put us on the first floor? Hand me the scissors! (*One of the lights moves.*)

Two Corpses:

Behold, we heard the trumpet sound, and we shook off death, and now we look out into an inferior light. Let's go back to bed.

Dead Novelist #2:

Sleep a thousand years, you lazy bones. Allow the gray hair to rest upon the yellow pillow.

Mouse #1:

I do not know what the commotion is about, but I will continue eating while the eating is good.

(*The pounding behind three of the remaining four holes persists. The director stands up and starts, inaudibly, to yell. The man who slides the cork stops working altogether, and sits on the unfinished cork to smoke a cigarette. The slaves and taskmasters flee the corks raining on stage.*)

Man Who Slides the Cork:

(*Yelling to the director*) Some fine play you have here.

(*Three corks tumble to the ground. One rolls off the stage. A man with a cane walks away from a hole and sits down in a chair. He puffs lightly on his cigar and talks to a man lying on a couch.*)

Dead Psychiatrist:

There, now, I have let in some light. That should cheer you up a bit.

Patient:

Yes, it does. Thank you.

Dead Psychiatrist:

Now, tell me again about this dream.

Patient:

I keep having the same dream in which everything is dark and a poem is
        constantly being recited.

Dead Psychiatrist:

Did the poem rhyme, or make reasonable sense?

Patient:

Why, yes, it did rhyme, and yes, it was reasonable.

Dead Psychiatrist:

Then certainly it is of the Devil. You must disregard such a dream.

(The light shifts.)

Famous Actor #1:

Cowboys and Indians. Now, that is something this land never will grow
        tired of watching. This play, on the other hand, won't work.

Famous Actor #2:

Car crashes. Timeless.

Famous Actor #1:

You know, I think this play would translate better in black and white.
        Color does not bode well.

Famous Actor #2:

Rebellion, I say. It needs more rebellion.

*(The noise grows increasingly louder. Musicians are talking with authors, actors with
railroad workers. Corpses complain about the bedlam. The mice eat, etc.)*

Director:

Enough! Enough! I'm pulling the plug on this rehearsal. Lights!

(The lights turn on all over the stage and auditorium. Rehearsal ends.)

Director:

(To assistant) Please go on stage and see what they need. I cannot deal with
        these actors.

(Assistant leaves. Director puts his head in his hands.)

Two Assistants:

Oh, how marvelous. How absolutely marvelous. The play will be a big hit.
We are certain.

Director:

Not right now, you two.

Two Assistants:

It will revolutionize the drama. We are certain.

Director:

(Loudly) Not now, I say! Save the flattery for someone who cares.

Two Assistants:

(Quietly and apprehensively, to each other) Well, it will. Oh, yes, Mr. Grumpy
Pants, it certainly will. *(A quiet laugh to each other)*

Director:

(Pulling his hair) Close the curtain. Close it, now. I don't want to look at the
monstrosity for which I am responsible. Close that curtain.

(Curtain closes three-fourths of the way, but then stops.)

Director:

(To himself) What have I done? What have I done?

(Assistant returns with the actors' list of demands.)

Director:

Well? What went wrong? What do those sniveling prima donnas want?

Assistant:

The musicians are angry because they say their lines do not do justice to
their parts. They want complete control over what they say, or
they will sue. The mice want some milk in their hole, but other
than that are fine and do not mind working overtime, and the
blind man seeks justice. The two Dead Novelists will not work
with the living author or his *baboons* (their word, not mine). The
corpses' only request is for pillows. The worst complainant is the
man who slides the cork. He seeks double pay for such steadily
hazardous work, weekends off, and a back brace.

Director:

(Angrily) Weekends off! Double the pay! He is my rock. He is intended to
epitomize constant effort, and here he is complaining about
wages. This is too much. And, what of the religious folk? Does
the prophet need a recliner, so his arthritic knees don't ache?
Should I request a masseuse for his knotted back?

Assistant:

Actually, sir, I never reached the religious hole. Among the fracas, it was
the only hole that remained plugged.

Director:

Oh, no. I forgot about them. Go quickly, and have the ladder raised.

Assistant:

Will do.

Two Assistants:

If there is nothing else we can do today, sir, may we be excused? Yes, I
have to pick up the kids, and still have to retrieve my dog from
the sitter. She gets angry when I am late.

Director:

(*With a superfluous wave of his hand*) Be gone, the two of you.

Two Assistants:

Until tomorrow. Adieu.

(*Actors file out, some waving goodbye. The auditorium is still. Director sits again with
his head in his hands. Female assistant returns*)

Assistant:

They have been freed. I have let them go until tomorrow, sir.

Director:

Thank you, dear. I don't know what I would do without you. Tell me,
kindly, what went wrong today?

Assistant:

Honestly?

Director:

Brutal honesty.

Assistant:

Well, I think your concept is solid. But I think it would be easier if you
had only a protagonist that happens to bump into these people.
That way, it would seem more like real life.

Director:

Real life is more complex than this play.

Assistant:

Yes, but the surroundings and perplexities are familiar. Here, I think even
the actors are influenced by the scene's strangeness.

(*Remaining cast and crew shout goodnights as they exit. The lights are turned off, save one on stage.*)

Assistant:

Come on, sir. Let me walk you home. We'll get this play right tomorrow morning.

Director:

No. Not tonight, my dear. I want to sit a while. I'll turn off the light. You go ahead.

Assistant:

Are you sure?

Director:

Yes. I am sure. Thank you.

(*He reaches up to clasp her hand in a gesture that says, "thanks for understanding." She reciprocates his look, and he releases her hand.*)

Director:

Have a good night.

Assistant:

You, too.

(*Assistant leaves. The auditorium is now abnormally silent after such an eventful day. Director sits for a time. After a while, his assistant returns with a hot meal. They eat and talk. The food restores some of the director's happiness. He is thankful for the woman. She leaves, this time for good.*)

Director:

(*To himself*) She was right.

(*An hour passes. He remains seated. Who knows what he thinks? Suddenly, something within the cheese stirs.*)

Director:

Who is here? Speak, whomever you are.

Man Who Slides the Cork:

Oh, I didn't realize anyone was still here. I was just returning to sleep.

Director:

To sleep?

Man Who Slides the Cork:

Yes. I have no home. No place to call my own. Nowhere to lay my weary head. Your assistant was kind enough to let me sleep here, as long as no one found out.

Director:

How did this happen?

Man Who Slides the Cork:

One does not know exactly how things come about anymore than one
knows how a tree grows. We can explain the scientific process,
but the wonder of it is too profound to fathom. In life, mysteries
abound.

Director:

Very well. I didn't mean to disturb you. Go ahead and sleep.

Man Who Slides the Cork:

Would you mind turning off the stage light? It is hard to sleep with that
thing shining.

Director:

I would hate to trouble you. Let me get that.

(*Director leaves his seat and turns off the light. He waits for his eyes to adjust, and
then sits down in the back row. Moth leaves its veiled corner and approaches the
director. In darkness, the man sees nothing but a vague shadow.*)

Director:

(*Jokingly*) One more come to snuff out my glory and prey upon my
essence. Too cowardly to come in the day, eh? Here is my shirt
sleeve, made from the finest wool. Dig in, you winged vampire.

Moth:

Flutter-flutter-patter-patter.

*I seek nothing from you. Oddly enough, I do not know why I have stopped near you,
unless I am compelled by a kind of compassion.* Flutter-flutter-patter-
patter.

Director:

Why do you hover before my face, shadow? The humming of your wings
sounds like hell's very laughter. Leave me. I am too old and tired
to fight. Laugh away, you incarnate devil. Let your wings spout
their furious laughter in my face. Such mockery, I will not
answer.

Moth:

Drum-drum-drum-drum.

The sound is but the sound of sadness. Please don't misunderstand. All have
misunderstood. Do you not see I am a bearer of light, not darkness?
Drum-drum-drum-drum.

Director:

There is not room for both of us. Either you go, or I must.

Moth:

Sad-drum-weighted-patter-melancholy-flutter.

I will go. I will hurry on to my death. Fleeting-flutter-distant-drum-faint-patter.
(Moth exits the auditorium. Perturbed director eventually falls asleep as he listens to
the loud snoring of the man who slides the cork.)

Moth:

*Such a play does not end. One simply closes the curtain...*the creature thought
upon this phrase, and so many other things, as it took to the
dotted night. In the sky, the North Star shone bright. It was a
welcome sight for a creature that does not like darkness. With
labored strokes, the creature headed due west. Off in the
distance, glistening like a metallic ribbon, lay the river, and just
beyond, the old man. How far the creature had come; what
strange places and people it had seen.

II

Some estimates date the moth at nearly 140 million years of evolutionary age, predating the butterfly by roughly 40 million. The moth, and butterfly, for that matter, compose the fourth-largest insect family— Lepidoptera, translated literally as "scale wings." Perhaps this is why the moth is met with vehement apprehension, and is responsible for such human misgivings. Scales are associated with reptiles, reptiles associated with dragons, and dragons with evil; much of modern mythology is encapsulated in man slaying the loathsome dragon. And, was it not scales that fell from the prophet's eyes, allowing him to see? These suspicions, coupled with most moths' infatuation with flying only at night and their strange skirmishes against light, evoke a deep-seated hatred. But, not all moths are only active at night, albeit those that travel by day are less common, and even though the butterfly is of the same family and oftentimes impossible to distinguish from the moth, the moth alone bears the wrath of errant human perception.

Truth be told, the scales, the target of such ill repute, actually grant the moth its color. Layer upon layer of shingle etched in variegated hues of pigment combine to form the heralded brilliant and distinctive patterns. But, this is not all. These pigmented and rigged scales actually refract light. It is light bouncing off scales in myriad directions that evinces such dazzling and iridescent colors. The moth, more so than any other creature, relies upon light to mystify man. So necessary is the light for these creatures that they must bathe in the sun's rays and warm their bodies before they can take to the sky. Without light, a moth would shrivel and die, and what a curious death it is.

Not only do its scales slowly fall off, leaving the moth lacking color and a way to gather light, but this deterioration causes the moth to lose warming faculties, and when its core temperature cannot be maintained, the moth can no longer live. Not all, but most moths slip into a comatose state when the ensuing night dips their core temperature below the life-sustaining minimum. Night lulls them into an infinite sleep.

III

Suffice to say, when the misunderstood creature left the strange
building with the neon glow out front, and when it saw the distant river
winding as a silver ribbon, excitement gripped the moth, and it longed to
make it back to the old man's side, but it doubted whether it possessed
the necessary proclivity to make it such a distance. The creature wondered
how deep the old man had dug. It wondered whether he was still digging,
or if he had given up. It wondered what he had found. It wondered if the
man would know how irresolute and how floundering its faith had
become once it left his side. All these wonderings caused such harrowing
pain and anxiety within the creature's abdomen that it wished to speed up
its return. But, gaining momentum was impossible. Its wings' scales had
begun to, and were presently, flaking off at a terminal rate. The creature
flew as far as it could, then alighted on an inviting limb and slept near the
water's edge.

Morning had stretched her ubiquitous cape far and wide, and the
noon sun had commenced its rounds when the creature roused. It slept
longer than it had wished, and, upon waking, found itself yet unrevived
and with an aching pressure against its lungs. The creature looked out
over the water, too weak to attempt a crossing. It began coughing
feverously and felt its insides shift and grumble to the call of death's
prattle. It would not make it through another night. It knew the river
would remain a barrier between it and the old man. Now, it didn't want
much. Perhaps a quiet corner in which to rest its wearied body; maybe
some company that wasn't abhorrent, and if luck might grant it a window
facing the sunset so it could a final time watch the giant orb sink, the
creature would be satisfied.

At 12:21 p.m., the creature flew along the river's edge and amongst
the houses and hotels crowding its banks. After hours of searching and
resting and then finding itself too tired to continue, the creature entered

an open door to a quaint hotel with a tilted sign that read "Port o' Call." The creature fluttered through the foyer, around men in strange uniforms, up a wooden staircase, and along the third-floor hallway. One room's door was ajar, a garbage can wedged as a doorstop. The creature entered the room and found four men sitting around a small table. They were talking quietly, discussing something that seemed important. Three of the men appeared to be ghosts or non-human, for they cast a surreal glow, constellation-like. The other man looked all-too human, worn out, droopy skin, emaciated cheeks, and eyes that appeared older and deeper than the ocean's prodigious abyss. Beyond the men, two large windows hung wide open, and diaphanous curtains, made from a white silky blend, blew inward and flapped like a dove's giant wings. Outside, the river could be seen, and up in its sky the sun began its descent. The creature flew toward the windows and crashed heavily on the left windowsill. The wind felt good against its wings and body, even though its force sent tiny shingles, too small to be perceived by the human eye, dashing in all directions. Here—here was a place for the creature to watch its last sunset and peacefully disintegrate when night came.

The sky's azure tones were tinctured by a regal purple as legion clouds began to congregate and form makeshift awnings for the gods' diurnal event. Tiny veins between the clouds appeared freckled with honey blood and infinitesimal floating violet globs. The sun drooped, and invisible hands seemed to let go of it in the same manner the affluent magnanimously drops a coin into a poor beggar's hat, so, to, the river appeared to be claiming this celestial coin and the transaction, this union, amalgamated the two, for the river burned gilded as the sun, except the gold appeared speckled, flecked like many shattered rays of golden light.

The four men vacated the small table and ambled toward the window. The creature remained still, so as not to disturb. The three men stood directly above it, but they were not looking at the threshold; their eyes were fixed on the sinking sun. The creature thought, ironically enough, that it could feel the sun reflecting off their white uniforms. It did not know whether the warmth was truly resultant upon the men, or whether it could be attributed to the anesthetic and hallucinogenic feeling of approaching death.

The three men did not murmur a word. The fourth stood at the other window, but his squinted gaze upon the still-brilliant sun suggested less tranquility. For a period of time, silence dominated. Finally, the fourth man turned toward the other three, and, in a still and soothing voice, asked: "How long?"

The three did not move, did not stir, did not turn their heads in the least, but the man in the middle whispered, in an assuming tone, all the while his eyes fixed on the descending sun: "It cannot be long, now."

The other two responded: "No, it cannot be much longer."

The three watched as the sun's circle touched the river's surface, reflecting onto the water in the shape of a bloated hourglass. The sinking sun had turned a brilliant orange and could be looked at directly.

"My, it is beautiful, isn't it?" whispered the man in the middle.

"My, it is," the other two answered almost unconsciously.

"One never tires of watching the sun," uttered the man on the left.

"No. One never tires of watching the sun," echoed the other two.

The sun was now a half-circle, and the sky, along with the clouds, mazed like fields of flamed tulips.

"Though it dies tonight, tomorrow it will rise again," confessed the man on the right.

"Though it dies tonight, it will live again," reiterated the other two in unison.

The three then grew somber and watched the phoenix sun in peace. When the creature looked back, they were gone. The creature could not say whether they vanished, or if they were ever really there; its mind had been disjointed since awakening that morning, and their discussion seemed scripted, not the way humans would speak. Though the three had witnessed the sunset up until a point, or if at all, they had abandoned the creature and the fourth man long before the spectacle's finale.

The fourth man moved from the right window to the left, and looked down at the little creature. "Hello, my friend. Come to watch the sunset, have you?"

The creature, with the boldness of the dying—what is left to lose— answered the man: "That I have, and I understand it is my last."

The words left the creature's mouth almost before it perceived it had spoken. Finally, and ironically too late, the creature had re-achieved its capacity for communication. But, even now, it thought to itself, *He will not understand. He is like the rest.*

But the man did understand, and responded, "Then what a resplendent last it is."

The creature was overjoyed. At last, someone who could comprehend. The tragedy of the mooted moment, as is so often the case, lay only in poor timing.

"What brings you here," asked the man.

"I was trying to return to an old friend before my life expires," replied the creature.

"Why did you leave this old friend in the first place," the man questioned.

The creature ventured to tell its story from start to finish as the man patiently listened. It told of the old man's quest to find reason beyond the root of suffering, of his noble aspiration to search underneath the pain. It spoke of its quest to broadcast the singular man's incorrigible and indomitable zeal of digging to reach the bottom of all existential groaning. It told of the horrible and sad people it continually bumped up against. It spoke of its unsteadied faith, how when it thought about the man it felt firm in its convictions, but when it allowed other worries to occupy its simple brain, it could not remember its goal. It told of so much more, and how, now that it had ventured into the unremitting world, all it hoped for was to make it back to the old man, to die at his slovenly feet, but, on the cusp, the tragic creature knew it would die without crossing the final threshold.

The man shook his head for a moment, and then asked the creature: "And what worries do you have now that you will sleep and wake no more?"

The creature thought for a moment about its fears, and, strangely enough, a sense of peace filled its entire being and allayed all preoccupations except two: "Would the old man be proud? Was I worthy of my task? Besides these," murmured the creature, "I have no regrets."

"Ah," said the man as a contemplative gesture of thought.

"And what did you find most difficult to overcome? What, above all else, did the world require of you?"

The creature considered his question. Its mind was slowing and it could feel its blood turning metallic; it felt the sluggish and vitiate clinking of its coggish heart, but it answered. "I suppose endurance was the attribute most required, and, yet, the hardest thing to prove worthy of maintaining."

The man looked at the creature, wiped his hand over his mouth, and muttered, "Endurance? Huh." The man reflected on the creature's answer, and then marveled at something else. "You have gone it alone with no guide?"

The creature answered with all the tenacity it could muster, "Memory led every thrashing of these wasted wings, every beat of this dying heart."

The man's furrowed brow straightened as he asked his next question. "What memory?"

The creature tired and had trouble speaking. "The farther I ventured from the old man…the more vivid the memory of his loving kindness, even when in the act of betraying the trust he placed in me…I felt his presence… spurring me onward."

The creature started to wheeze and its chronic lung began to fill with fluid. It felt a violent chill wrench its innards.

"Come," said the man, smiling, "Let's watch the sun one final time."

The two looked at the quarter of remaining sun. It shone incarnadine and transformed into a fierce stripe, a sanguine gash painted beneath the warrior's undaunted eye in preparation for a battle where imminent death lurks all across the battlefield. The sun had melded with the river, and the line where one ended and the other began was imperceptible. The caravan clouds, vertiginously outstretched from the sun, uncoiled their majestic carpets before their dying king.

The river gleamed black as night and the sun reflected sparkling embers, cast from the perishing hearth, to choke in the oily darkness. Then, the sun slivered crimson. Without looking at the creature, the man whispered, almost inaudibly: "It's hard to know such things, but I wonder if you will yet see greater things than this, creature."

With dolorous eyes, the creature watched the sinking of the somnolent sun. It took in one last wisp of light, thought of the land it would see no more, thought again about its decision to ever leave the man's side, and silently gave up the withered ghost.

The man watched as the tiny sliver of sun, the clinging heartbeat on a monitor, took one last beat and then flatlined, disappeared, leaving only the half-life of an effervescent glow on the horizon where it last shone. Darkness had begun its crawl. The creature's casing lay cold and stiff. The man looked down and sighed. He went to the doorway, retrieved the garbage can, shut the door, and walked back toward the window. He put the trashcan underneath the creature and looked at it one last time.

"What does a moth know about endurance?" he sighed, as he swept the dead moth into the trashcan—a trashcan already littered with other moths. The man returned the trashcan to its usual position, then walked to the window to peer out.

The sweltering darkness is deepening. The abiding light is past and gone. Eventide cloaks the land and the day's ephemeral glories passed.

"Tomorrow, I will do it again," said the man into the bland darkness. "Ad infinitum, if need be."

But the darkness did not hear, nor was it listening, the man knew. He goes over to the trashcan and looks at the creature's corporeal coffin. At the bottom of the trashcan, the creature lies indiscernible. Amid so many dead moths, a gleam reflects off the few remaining scales on the creature's wings still shining, but signifying little. It might have been a simple trick of the light, nothing more. The man puts the trashcan back down.

He then closes and draws the blinds on both windows. In darkness, he walks over to a bed. He kneels. He says a silent prayer. He pulls the sheets back, sits on the bed, swings his feet up and around, places them under the covers, pulls the covers up to his chest, turns on his side, flattens the pillow, rests his head, and within five minutes is fast asleep. The man has done the same thing for so long it has become routine. No amount of one day's bizarreness could change his nightly custom. He will soundly sleep until morning. Outside, and beating against the windows, the frantic wind howls, yet the man is aware of nothing but his dream, nothing but sleep.

ALEC BRYAN lives in Utah and curses every winter. To view a list of his publications and writings, visit **www.alecbryan.com**.

CPSIA information can be obtained at www.ICGtesting.com
Printed in the USA
240931LV00001B/38/P

9 780982 673423